"Poor girl!" Molly croons, kneeling beside the injured filly. "How long have you been here?" Molly is horrified to see the mustang's lackluster eyes and swollen tongue.

But even if she can save the little filly, Molly knows her father will never let her keep a wild horse.

What can she do?

Prairie Lady

Original title: Prairie Wind

by SHARON WAGNER

Illustrated by Joseph Cellini

SCHOLASTIC BOOK SERVICES
NEW YORK • TORONTO • LONDON • AUCKLAND • SYDNEY • TOKYO

Chapter 1

Molly Rogers brushed her short dark hair back quickly, not bothering to look in the mirror. She knew too well what she would see — a too thin face and wistful eyes. Only the sight of a horse, or her good friend Dan, could turn that wistful look into a smile. Molly was thirteen, but small for her age. In her worn jeans and cotton shirt she looked even smaller.

She went to the window to look out at the bright, early June morning. Already the sunshine was sparkling on the fresh, green buffalo grass. From the kitchen below she could hear the familiar banging of pots and pans, and now and again the sound of her parents talking. Molly lingered at the window a moment longer, then hurried downstairs toward the tempting smell of bacon and eggs and fresh-baked bread.

"I was just about to call you," her mother said, as Molly entered the kitchen. "Will you put the milk on the table, Molly, please?"

"Yes, and good morning," Molly said, getting the milk pitcher out of the refrigerator.

"Hi, princess," her father said. "What are you going to do today?"

"Oh, I don't know. Go walking, I guess."

"Would you like to ride into town with me?" he asked. "I've got to pick up some supplies."

"No, I don't think so," Molly answered, beginning to feel uncomfortable.

"Why don't you want to go in, dear?" her mother asked.

"I just don't feel like it today," Molly said. This wasn't strictly true; she *never* wanted to go into town anymore.

"You really should start going into town more often," her mother insisted. "You could meet some of the boys and girls you'll be going to school with in the fall."

The bacon sandwich Molly had made for herself suddenly tasted like sawdust, but she chewed at it doggedly and finally managed to finish it. "I'll go in next time," she promised, getting up from the table. "Excuse me," she said, "I'd better do my chores."

As Molly went through the laundry room at the back of the kitchen, she heard her mother say, "Jack, I'm worried about her. She doesn't have any friends now that Linda's moved away."

Molly hurried so she wouldn't have to hear anymore. She couldn't explain to her parents how she felt, that she didn't want to face the boys and girls in town. They were so self-assured, they made her feel shy and self-conscious.

Feeding the chickens and the stock in the barn didn't take long, and Molly soon had the day's collection of eggs stored away. Her morning chores completed, she called to Baron and set off toward the distant mountain. Her walks rarely went anywhere, but they gave the aging sheep dog a chance to stretch his legs and gave Molly an excuse to escape her mother's kind, but embarrassing questions. And sometimes, on these walks, Molly would catch a glimpse of some wild horses in the distance.

From the top of the rise behind the

house, she could see the little white-painted schoolhouse, the only school she had ever known. For eight years she had gone to that one-room school with the same twenty students. And now, this fall, she would be going to the high school in town. Molly groaned. How could she fit into Medford High, along with five hundred students — all strangers? Usually, just leaving the house was enough to make Molly forget her troubles, but today it didn't work, not until Baron began barking up ahead.

In a moment a large jackrabbit bounded toward Molly, then vanished behind a clump of grass. The old sheep dog followed, sniffing curiously until he located the burrow. Molly let him whine and dig for a few minutes, then called him away.

They continued on toward the mountains in the quiet of the morning, broken only by Baron's panting and the whisper of the prairie wind.

When they topped a higher rise of ground, Molly caught sight of some animals grazing on the far side of the creek that flowed across her father's ranch. For a moment she thought they were some of her father's cattle, then she remembered that the herd had not yet been moved up

4

from the winter pasture. That meant they might be horses . . .

"Heel, Baron," she ordered, starting down the hill slowly. Her father did not run horses on his land, so these horses must be wild. Molly counted twenty full-grown horses and almost a dozen foals. It wasn't the first time she'd seen a wild herd, but this one was close — closer than usual. They were probably from the Indian reservation on the western boundary of her father's ranch. There were few fences on the reservation and some horses always managed to escape the roundups the Indians held every spring and fall.

"Baron," Molly said softly. "Stay here. Lie down and stay here."

The dog flopped down obediently. Baron had been a working sheep dog until he grew too old to herd a flock. Although Molly had only had him for a year, he obeyed her well. She was sure he wouldn't follow her and accidentally frighten the herd. She set off slowly, stepping carefully and trying not to stir the grass and bushes.

It took almost an hour for her to work her way to the creek. Once there, she was less than a hundred yards from the herd.

Her heart pounded with excitement as she parted the new leaves and took a close look at the wild herd.

Disappointingly, the horses were a scrubby lot. Except for the scarred old stallion, who was their leader, they were still patched with long winter hair, and their manes and tails were matted with twigs and dried mud. They cropped the grass steadily and soberly. They were still lean from the winter. Only the foals, rolling or sleeping contentedly under their mothers' watchful eyes, seemed to be enjoying the spring sunshine.

Even so, Molly could see that several of the mares were of good stock. Under their shaggy hair and unkempt manes she recognized the good bones and fine heads of the thoroughbreds. She wondered why their owners had left them to run free.

Suddenly one of the mares lifted her head and flipped her ears nervously. With a snort, the stallion immediately plunged into a gallop, cutting swiftly around the herd and sending all the horses into full retreat. They were almost out of sight when Molly heard Baron's deep bark. She tried to locate the sound, a little surprised and disappointed that the dog had disobeyed her.

Chapter 2

It didn't take her long to discover that the barking came from upstream, not back where she'd left Baron. Molly thought of just calling him, now that the horses were gone, but there was a note of urgency in his bark that drew her on. When she pushed aside the last barrier of brush and slender branches, shock brought her to a halt.

One of the wild horses hadn't been able to run away. At first Molly thought the horse was dead, but when Baron ran past the animal, she saw a quiver of fear stir the dead-looking brown hide.

"Down, Baron. Quiet boy." She patted the dog absently, her eyes on the horse. Cautiously, she approached.

The horse was a small filly, not over three years old, she guessed. Molly looked around, piecing the story together from the filly's position and the torn-up earth in the clearing. An old rope still cut into the raw flesh of the horse's neck. The frayed end was securely caught between a rock outcropping and the weathered trunk of a birch tree.

Some time ago the filly had been roped, but she had broken free, trailing the rope behind her as she ran with the wild herd. When she came into the clearing to graze, the rope had caught. The scarred turf showed how violently she had fought to be free.

"Poor girl," Molly said, kneeling beside the filly's head. "I'll bet you were awfully scared, but you shouldn't have fought so hard. You just hurt yourself more."

The filly shivered a little, but showed no other sign of life. Looking closely, Molly saw the lackluster eyes and then the swollen tongue. "How long have you been here, girl?" Molly talked quietly as she freed the rope, checking the noose to be sure the horse wasn't being choked. The filly shivered again, though her hide was hot and dry.

"Water," Molly said, suddenly realizing

that the filly was dying of thirst though she was not more than thirty feet from the creek. Molly looked around but there was nothing in the small clearing that she could use to carry water. "Come on, horse," she said, tugging on the rope, "you've *got* to get up."

The sunken eyes rolled at her a little, and the filly managed to lift her head a few inches off the ground. "That's the girl, I'll help you," Molly said. But the horse was too weak, and in a moment her slender muzzle was back on the dusty earth.

"Oh, Baron." Tears of frustration stung Molly's eyes. The dog whined softly as though he understood her anguish. "We can't just let her die here," Molly said, bending down to stroke the delicate head.

"Won't you try again?" she pleaded. "It's not far, really." But even as she asked it, Molly knew that it was hopeless. The filly had used all her strength in the battle with the rope, and without food and water she was too weak even to struggle. The thirty feet might as well be thirty miles to the filly. She'd given up and was now just waiting to die.

"If only I had something to bring you

some water in," Molly said, thinking out loud. "If you just had some water, maybe you could get up." She didn't want to go to the ranch for help; she felt the filly might not live long enough for her to get back.

"Say, I've got an idea." Molly stood up and began unbuttoning her shirt. She pulled it off as she ran to the creek, feeling shy even though she was sure no one could see her. She dipped the shirt into the cold water and carried it, dripping, back to the horse.

"Now, how does that feel?" she asked, squeezing the shirt slowly over the filly's swollen tongue. A lot of the water ran away and was wasted in the prairie soil, but after three trips, the filly could close her mouth again. Another half dozen trips and the horse was wet from head to tail. Molly sank down beside her again.

"How about it, horse?" she asked. "Ready to try to get up? I can't bring you enough water this way and . . ." Molly stopped as another thought crossed her mind, a memory from past summers.

She and Linda Henderson had been best friends through all the summers she could remember. Their special place, where they had met almost every summer day, was the pool in the creek, where the water came down off the rocks. In her mind, Molly could still see the cave they'd discovered behind the falls. It had been their hideout when they played settlers and Indians. It was their dollhouse, and their refuge from the world. If she remembered correctly, there was still a battered pail lying there that had been part of their pioneering equipment.

Molly shook out her shirt and pulled it on hastily, shivering a little as the cold, wet material touched her bare skin. "I'll be right back, horse," she said. "Just hang on a little longer, please."

It wasn't far to the falls, but Molly ran fearfully, haunted by the thought that the horse might die while she was gone. She was such a small horse and she'd fought so hard. It weighed heavily on Molly's heart to think that she might have found her too late to save her life.

When Molly reached the falls, she was surprised to see how different they looked with the heavy flow of melted snow pouring down from the mountains. It took precious minutes for Molly to locate the narrow ledge that was the only entrance to the cave. The ledge was slimy with moss,

of the water nearly pushed
into the swirling pool below. By the
time she reached the cave, she was soaking
and one of her fingernails was torn from
her desperate hold on the rocks.

The cave seemed smaller than she remembered, and it was so dark she had a
hard time finding the narrow ledge where
they'd always kept their few dishes and
other possessions. Everything was just as
they'd left it the day Linda moved away.
For a moment Molly felt again the pains of
loneliness; then she pushed the memories
away and began searching for the pail.

She was about to give up when she
spotted it in the corner, half buried under
the winter's accumulation of dirt and peb-
bles. Hurriedly shaking them off, she ran
back to the narrow opening and began inch-
ing her way back along the moss-coated
ledge. Twice her foot slipped, but she clung
grimly to the pail and dug her rock-bruised
fingers into the tiny crevices to keep her
balance. Baron greeted her happily when
she reached dry ground and they ran back
through the trees together.

The filly was just as they'd left her, but
Molly felt better when she saw that the

horse was still breathing. She took the pail to the creek and filled it. It was battered and rusty, but when she lifted it, no water leaked out. She set it down beside the filly with a sigh of relief.

"There you go, girl," she said. "Drink a little of that, then we'll see about getting you some grass to eat."

The filly stirred and her nostrils quivered, but after a moment she lay still again. Her eyes were on Molly and they were full of pleading, but it was obvious that she was too weak to drink the life-giving water. Was it too late? Molly asked herself. Was the filly doomed in spite of everything she'd tried to do?

"You've got to try," she said. "I'll help you, but you've got to drink it yourself if you want to live."

She knelt beside the horse, pulling the pail over against her knee. Then, lifting the filly's head up, she moved in closer until the filly's whole neck was off the ground. The horse didn't fight her, but she didn't help either. With a prayer, Molly slipped the horse's muzzle into the water.

For a long moment nothing happened, then, convulsively, the filly began to swallow. "Good girl," Molly said. "Good girl!" She didn't even notice the tears running down her cheeks.

When the pail was half empty, Molly pushed it away. "I'm sorry, girl," she said, lowering the filly's head to the ground, "but I can't let you have too much at once. You rest for a while, then you can have some more."

By the time the filly had finished her second pail of water, Molly no longer had to hold up her head. The horse had folded her slender legs under her and had rolled over enough to keep her head up. Molly began pulling up grass and piling it in front of her. The filly sniffed at it, but wasn't ready to eat for a long time. Even when the sun was well over toward the western mountains, the filly was still not strong enough to get up. She could never make the long walk back to the ranch house.

"I hate to leave you here, horse," Molly said, "but I'm going to have to. My folks will be worried anyway, because I didn't come home for lunch."

The filly's eyes, brighter now, watched Molly gather grass in the clearing. "She doesn't look like the same horse," Molly thought with satisfaction. Though still bone thin and fragile looking, no one would mistake her now for a dead or dying horse.

When the grass was piled high enough to satisfy her, Molly untangled the rope and fashioned it into a halter. "I'm going to tie you," she told the filly, "just in case you find out you can get up. I want you to be here when I come back for you tomorrow."

She refilled the pail and set it near enough for the filly to reach. "You can get to the creek," Molly explained, "if you do get up. But if you can't make it, that should be enough water for tonight."

With one last pat, she reluctantly left the filly, calling Baron to heel. Now that the horse was settled and safe, Molly's hunger began knifing at her stomach. It had been a long, busy time since breakfast, but she hadn't even felt hungry at noon. Now, however, she almost ran in her eagerness to tell her parents about the wild horses and the dainty filly she had already claimed for her own.

Chapter 3

The tantalizing smells of dinner met her at the door. Baron trotted in ahead, and went to his dish and whined. "Well, if it isn't a couple of hungry strays wandering in from the prairie," her mother said. "I was about to send out a search party. Where have you been all day?"

"Up toward the falls. There was this—"

"Not now. Set the table and feed your dog. Your father will be in from the barn in about five minutes, and I want to have dinner on the table for him."

Molly filled Baron's dish, then washed her hands, feeling all the excitement draining out of her. It was a different world here—

not the urgent sense of life or death she'd felt on the plains with the filly; but a subdued, and for her, often lonely existence in this quiet house. If only she had a brother or sister to share things with, Molly thought. It would ease the strain she felt at times like this, between herself and her parents.

Her father came in and sat down at the table. "Smells good, Annie," he said.

"I fixed the chicken the way you like it, dear." The warmth in their voices didn't ease Molly's sense of aloneness. But her physical hunger was so strong she could hardly keep her fingers away from the chicken as she carried the platter to the table.

"Say, you were gone a long time today. Where did you go, anyway?" Her father took the platter.

"I walked up toward the falls. There was a whole herd of wild horses up there and —"

"Oh, blast it!" her father broke in. "The fence must be down again."

"Maybe they swam the creek," Molly suggested, surprised at his outburst.

"Not during the spring flood. No, the

fence must be down. I'll get Dan to help me check it tomorrow, then you can help us run those mustangs back to the reservation."

"Why do they have to go back?" Molly asked. "I mean, they weren't hurting anything."

"They eat just as much grass as a useful animal, and they're completely worthless. Most of them should be sold to the cannery, anyway."

"Daddy!" Now Molly was shocked.

"Well, honey, they just aren't worth anything. Nobody lets their good stock run loose, so it's just scrubs or outlaws that make up the herds. They aren't even worth breaking."

"But there were some good horses in the herd, I saw them. I was real close today, Daddy."

"Oh, sure, a few good ones get loose, but they'll be caught in the spring roundup. Besides, once horses have run wild, it spoils them, I think. They aren't dependable anymore."

"You just don't like wild horses," Molly said, her hunger fading again as she thought of the helpless filly.

"I've never seen one I'd want to ride. Now pass the gravy please, Molly."

"Your daddy said there were a lot of youngsters your age in town today," her mother said, changing the subject. "You really should have gone with him."

Molly nodded and chewed mechanically, no longer tasting the crusty goodness of the chicken; her mind was on the filly. What could she do? The horse was too weak to run with the herd yet, and even if she were stronger . . . Molly thought of the gentle eyes and the new life that had come into them when the filly had drunk the water . . . Molly couldn't give her up now.

All evening she tried to find an opportunity to tell her parents about the filly, but somehow it never quite fit into the conversation. Besides, whenever she was ready to speak out, she'd think of her father's remark about the cannery and a lump would fill her throat. The filly was too important to her to take any risk. She went to bed without telling her parents about it.

Molly woke even before the sun rose, her mind alive with worry about the filly. She got up and dressed as quietly as possible. When her chores were done, she hid a basket of supplies just over the ridge, then went back to the house for breakfast.

"Aren't you the early bird," her mother said. "If I didn't know you better, I'd think you had a date out there somewhere."

"Oh, Mother." Molly felt her cheeks growing red and hated herself for blushing.

"Where are you going, anyway?" her father asked.

"Oh, just for a walk, like always." Molly kept her eyes on her plate.

"Why don't you come with us instead? Dan and I can always use some help riding fence."

"Maybe some other time, Daddy. I really do have some things I want to do today."

"Like what?" His tone was insistent.

"Well, I thought I'd go to the cave — remember, where Linda and I used to play. We left some stuff there and . . ." It didn't sound very convincing and Molly hated herself for making up such a story.

"I suppose you're going to look for the wild horses again," he said. "I can't see why you'd rather look at a bunch of shaggy mustangs than ride a decent horse and do something useful."

"I'm sorry, Daddy." Molly finished her

breakfast in silence and left as quietly as possible. This was no way to make her father want the filly, and yet, she couldn't go with him; the filly might need her. So many things could have happened during the night.

This time she headed directly for the creek, Baron trotting contentedly beside her. The basket contained a small halter, a small bag of oats, some salve for the welts the rope had made on the filly's neck, and a large pile of molasses cubes to tempt her appetite.

As she walked along, Molly's mind roamed ahead to another worry. How had the filly gotten the rope around her neck in the first place? Had she been roped while she was running with the herd, or had she escaped from some ranch? Did the filly already belong to someone? Molly searched her mind. She couldn't remember seeing a brand, but she'd been too worried about the filly to even look for one.

As she neared the creek, she was surprised to see that the horses were back. She'd seen nothing important about their choice of a grazing place before, but now that she had found the filly . . . Were the horses waiting for the filly to rejoin them? It was quite possible. Molly walked through the trees, not trying to sneak up on the herd, but hoping that she wouldn't frighten them too much.

The stallion bugled for his mares while she was still a long way from them. Molly paused to watch him gather his herd and send them galloping away. Scrubs or not, they looked beautiful and so free. Molly felt a pang of envy. They seemed to have no problems — the grass was plentiful, the streams were high and clear, there was warm sunshine and no work. They didn't have school or parents, or suffer from loneliness.

From the clearing ahead, she heard a heartbroken whinny that snapped her back from her dreaming and hurried her on her way. The filly was still alive, but not at all happy. Molly, fearing the filly would tangle herself in the rope trying to follow the herd, reached the clearing in record time. To her surprise, she found the filly lying just as she had left her.

"Well, little lady," Molly said softly, stopping to catch her breath before she approached the horse, "how do you feel today?"

The filly turned toward Molly, flipping her delicate ears back and forth uncertainly. Her eyes were brighter now and her coat seemed less dull, but she made no attempt to get to her feet. Molly walked up to her slowly, noting that the water bucket was empty and the grass stacks had disappeared.

"You look better," she observed, pausing to let the filly sniff her outstretched hand before she tried to touch her. She set the basket down and took the pail to the creek to refill it. The filly drank thirstily, then watched with interest as Molly dug in the basket for a molasses cube.

"Taste these, girl," she said, offering the filly one. "They will make you forget your wild friends. You're going to be my horse from now on, and I promise it won't be all work."

The filly took the cube daintily, her velvet lips barely brushing Molly's hand. Molly untied the rope halter and buckled on the leather one she'd brought from the barn. The filly watched her with interest, accepting the petting and the molasses cubes without fear.

"Now," Molly said, "it's time for you to

get up. You can't lie here forever. Come on." She pulled lightly on the halter.

At first the filly seemed to be cooperating. She straightened her front legs until she was in a sitting position, but got no farther. "Come on," Molly repeated, pulling on the halter. The horse had her hind legs tucked under her in the proper position, but though she tried to get up, she couldn't. After a few moments, she folded her front legs under her again, lying down as she had been when Molly arrived.

"Poor girl," Molly said, kneeling beside her, "what's the matter?"

Molly examined the filly's hind legs and haunches for injuries. It took only a few moments to discover what was keeping the horse down. She was lying on her left side and her left hind fetlock and pastern were hot and swollen. She shuddered when Molly touched her leg or tried to move it out so she could examine it.

A hollow fear grew inside Molly. Had she saved the filly from one death only to lose her to another? Had the slender leg been broken during the filly's frantic battle with the rope? The joint and pastern showed raw rope burns in the swollen flesh, proving that the leg had been tangled. Molly tried to feel for a break, but the joint was too swollen. Grimly, she took the rag she'd brought with her and began tearing it in two.

She dipped both rags in the creek, wringing one out but leaving the other dripping. This one she wrapped around the swollen ankle. While she waited for the cold water to ease the swelling, she washed the rope burns on the filly's neck and rubbed in the salve. As she worked, she tried not to think of the ankle. A horse with a broken leg had no future in the prairie country. Once in a while a very valuable horse could be saved, but a wild filly — even Molly could understand the mercy of a bullet.

By noon the swelling was much smaller, but Molly's gently probing fingers still told her nothing. The filly whickered when Molly pressed too hard or moved the leg, but otherwise tolerated the handling with surprising patience. Wild horse or not, Molly thought, the filly was a real lady.

As she fussed over the filly, another worry began to haunt Molly. Even if the filly's leg wasn't seriously hurt, the creek was no longer a safe place for her to stay.

The wild horses had come to be with her last night and probably would be returning again as soon as Molly left. That meant that she, Dan, and her father would be coming through here to round them up.

"I can't let him find you yet," Molly said. "He'd either run you back to the reservation or shoot you."

The filly nuzzled her arm, her eyes soft and trusting. "You've got to get up," Molly said. "I can hide you, but not here."

She tried again, urging the filly more strongly, but with the same results. The horse tried, but she had to put most of her weight on the bad fetlock to do so. She shuddered and flopped back down. As soon as Molly realized the hopelessness of it, she let go of the halter and sank down beside the filly, feeling weary and defeated enough to cry. She had tried so hard to save this horse and now it seemed doomed anyway.

"Maybe Daddy won't find you," Molly said, stroking the silky head. "Maybe the wild herd won't come back here tonight."

But Molly had little hope, remembering the way the filly had whinnied when the wild horses left her this morning. If her father heard that, he'd investigate, and there was no place here for Molly to hide the filly.

Mechanically, Molly changed the drying rag for a cold, wet one, and then fed the filly part of the oats she'd brought. "Prairie Lady," she said, testing the name. It seemed to fit. The filly was a child of the prairie and her behavior had certainly proved that she was a lady and not a rough mustang. "My Prairie Lady." The filly whickered quietly and Molly blinked back tears.

The day dragged on. Molly was hungry but afraid to go home. She knew her parents were angry with her for not riding fence. Going home would give them a chance to find something for her to do, something that would keep her from coming back. It was almost two o'clock when she figured out what she hoped was a solution to her present problem.

"Lady," she said, "I'm going to roll you over. Maybe if your good leg is under you, you can get up."

Rolling the filly over wasn't easy. Though she was a small horse and pitifully thin, she was far too heavy for Molly to handle. After a few minutes of trying, Molly realized it would take something more than her strength. She looked around and spotted the rope. It took only a moment to knot it around the filly's front legs. By running the rope around a sturdy birch tree behind the filly, Molly was able to pull Lady over on her back. The filly rolled the rest of the way herself.

Molly sank down, shaking from the strain of trying so hard, but as soon as she'd caught her breath, she hurried to untie Lady's legs; the filly shivered with the touch of the rope. Molly knew what cruel memories it had for Lady, and she sat for a while, just rubbing the dirt and grime from Lady's shoulder and talking to her.

"I'm sorry, Lady," she said, "but we have to try it this way. You rest now, then you've *got* to get up. It's our only chance."

The clearing was warm and buzzing with insects. Baron lay under a bush, sleeping, his legs twitching as he dreamed of the rabbits he'd been chasing. Molly leaned over the filly, wiping the crusted dirt off her side to search for a brand. She felt better when she saw that the thin brown sides were unmarked.

"Well, Lady," Molly said with a sigh, "I guess we'd better try. It's a long walk to the only place I can hide you."

This time it was harder just to get the filly to sit up with her front legs in the proper position, and when Molly tugged at the halter, Lady didn't respond. Her eyes looked pleadingly at Molly, as though she couldn't understand why she was being tortured.

"Come on, Lady," Molly begged. "Please try — for me." But it was no use. Lady remained in a sitting position, her ears turning back in anger now. Molly blinked away the tears, as she tugged stubbornly at the halter.

Just as she was ready to give up, her eyes lit on the sleeping dog, and a desperate idea came to her. "Baron," she called. "Baron, get her, boy! Get the horse!"

For a moment the old dog hesitated, as though he wasn't sure he'd understood the command. But when she repeated it, he came at a run, barking and snarling viciously. Molly pulled on the halter, which was nearly ripped from her fingers as the frightened filly plunged clumsily to her feet.

"Down, Baron," Molly shouted, and was relieved to see the dog drop instantly. "Good dog," she added, before turning to the trembling filly. "It's all right, Lady," she soothed. "He wouldn't hurt you, not really."

The filly swayed unsteadily on her slender legs. She seemed even smaller than when she was lying on the ground. Her ribs made ridges on her dusty sides and her hip bones were sharp points straining the thin hide. Fearfully, Molly took a step, leading her.

The walk to the creek was a shaky one; the horse limped badly and her three good legs were barely strong enough to carry her. Once at the creek, however, she drank deeply, then began grazing contentedly. Molly didn't rush her. The horse was limping, but she did seem to be putting a little weight on the injured leg when she walked, which meant it was probably only badly bruised and sprained.

Molly gathered up everything in the clearing, fed Lady a few more molasses cubes, then began to ease her away from the creek. She made no attempt to lead the horse, just enticed her along with the cubes and petting. It was a long way from the creek to the corral that Molly planned to use as a hiding place for her Lady.

Chapter 4

The corral that Molly was heading for was located near the northern edge of the ranch. It had been built into a canyon by old-time horse hunters as a trap for the wild herds. Her father never used it, and Molly was sure the filly would be safe there.

The walk from the creek to the small box-canyon corral would ordinarily have taken little more than an hour, but Lady began staggering if they didn't stop frequently. Molly kept a close watch on the injured fetlock and was pleased to note that Lady was using it more and more.

"Guess it was just like a sprained ankle, wasn't it, girl," she said. "I think you're going to be all right now. There's plenty of grass in the canyon and a deep pool of spring water. You can just rest and get fat and pretty; then I'll take you down to the ranch when you're all well. You're going to be my horse."

Whenever Baron loped by, looking for rabbits or gophers to chase, Lady trembled and shied, nearly falling in her effort to avoid the dog. Molly felt a twinge of guilt, knowing she'd been the one who had caused Lady's fear. "It's all right, Lady," she said, rubbing the flaring nostrils. "You'll have to get used to Baron. He won't hurt you."

The dog stopped when he heard his name and stood looking at them, his plume of a tail wagging with interest. For a moment Molly considered calling him over, but the filly's fear was so recent she decided to give her time to forget. "Go find a rabbit, Baron," she said, laughing at the seriousness with which the old dog began his sniffing hunt.

The sun was nearing the mountains when they finally reached the canyon corral. Molly led the filly through the open gate and over to the pool of spring-fed water.

There she poured the remaining oats in a rocky hollow and let the filly eat while she checked the fence. The canyon walls rose steep on three sides. The fence that closed the open end was still strong; the old posts, grayed by many winters, were firm and solid in the turf.

Several of the rails were tied in place with ropes. Molly smiled to see how well they'd stayed. She and Linda had set those rails; they'd seen the wild horses the summer before last and dreamed of driving the herd in here and choosing two to keep for their own. Molly looked back to where the filly stood, belly deep in the lush grass. Her own dream was now coming true.

The sliding bar that held the old gate shut was rotten and broke in her hands like cheese, but the rope that had gotten badly tangled in the first place, was fine for tying the gate shut. Molly went back to give the filly the rest of the molasses cubes and a few more pats.

"You'll be safe here," she said. "I may not be able to come tomorrow, but you have water and plenty of grass. Just eat and let your leg heal." One last pat and Molly climbed the fence and started for home.

When she looked back the filly was watching her. She whistled for Baron and walked on. Halfway through the big corral, she heard the whinny. It was as lonely as the one she'd heard when the wild horses galloped away from the creek.

Though Molly hurried until her side ached and her shirt was soaked with perspiration, it was twilight when she and Baron came in sight of the ranch house. It didn't make her feel any better when she saw three saddled horses tied to the corral rail. As she started down the hill, her parents and Dan, the hired man, came out of the house. Baron ran ahead, barking a greeting. Molly tried to run too, but her legs refused to move any faster.

"Where have you been?" her mother demanded when Molly stumbled down the hill to the corral.

"We were just getting ready to go out looking for you," her father said, the worry and relief plain on his face even in the dim light.

"I . . . a . . . got sort of delayed," Molly said, panting for breath and trying to think.

"I'd have thought you were lost if there was any place on this range that you didn't know." Her father's voice was sharp with anger now.

"Well, I saw the wild herd again and —"

"And you spent the whole day trailing that worthless bunch," her father finished for her.

Molly nodded, grateful that he'd saved her from telling a lie about the day. She hated to lie, but the filly still needed her protection; her very life might depend on it. "I went too far and it took so long to walk back and . . . I'm sorry you were so worried."

An uncomfortable silence fell over the group for a moment, then Dan, shuffling his feet, said, "Well, I'll unsaddle the horses, Jack. We won't be needing them now. Glad you're home, maverick."

"Me, too," Molly said gratefully. Dan hadn't called her maverick for quite a while and she sensed that it was his way of letting her know he was on her side, whatever she was doing.

"Well, you'd better come in and eat," her mother said. "I saved you a plate. If you don't start eating decently, the first good wind we have will blow you clear out of the state."

"I'm starved," Molly said as they started for the house. Evidently they really believed she had been following the wild herd, and Dan's quiet manner had eased the tension. She turned to her father and asked, "Did you find where the fence was down?"

"Just where Dan told me it would be," he said, opening the back door, "right north of the creek."

"How'd he know where to look?" Molly asked, though she knew what his answer would be.

"That I'll never know. Must be his Indian nature. I think he was born with a whole set of instincts the rest of us don't have."

"I used to think it was sort of spooky when he first came to work for us," her mother said. "But it sure does come in handy."

Molly laughed with them. "Like when he smells rain and tells you to take your clothes in?" she asked.

"He's only been wrong once in the fifteen years he's worked for us, and that time the wind blew the storm around us."

"I couldn't run the place without him,"

her father agreed. "He's better than two ordinary hands."

Molly patted Baron's head. She knew that she too would have had trouble running her world without Dan. When she was a little girl, he had seemed like the pictures she'd seen of Indian braves and chiefs — rather fierce and forbidding. But now she knew that his black eyes could warm with love, and that he didn't need to smile to laugh inside.

It had been Dan who had brought her two orphaned baby rabbits to take care of when she had the measles and couldn't leave her room. Dan had taught her to ride and to build snares that captured wild things without injuring them. His little one-room cabin had been her second home as soon as she was old enough to walk down to it. It was there that she'd learned to love all the wild prairie creatures, for Dan was never without a dozen or so animal companions.

"It's funny," her mother said, as she put Molly's supper on the table. "I was worried about you, but Dan seemed so sure that you were all right and that he could find you."

"He probably would have," Molly said,

wondering to herself just how much Dan had guessed about her and the filly.

"Well, I'll tell you one thing," her father said, "tomorrow you're going to go with us and stay with us. No more of this leaving after breakfast and being gone all day."

"You're too old for that," her mother agreed. "It's time you started acting and thinking like a young lady."

Molly bit back angry words, knowing that this was no time to start an argument. Dan had eased her homecoming and her parents hadn't questioned her any further about where she'd been, so silence was the safest course. Still, it hurt when her mother treated her like a child.

Molly thought of the filly and Dan's understanding till the sting faded from her mind and she could go on eating without really listening. She escaped to her room as soon as she could and spent the rest of the evening reading the few books she had on horse training, and dreaming of her future with Prairie Lady.

Chapter 5

The morning dawned gray and cold. Molly shivered her way to the window. She was used to the swiftly changing weather of Montana and was not surprised to see that the clouds hung low and heavy over the plains, obscuring the mountain peaks and graying the summer green of the landscape.

Her first thoughts were of the filly. It would be cold and wet in the canyon. How she wished that Lady could be safe and warm in the barn with the other horses instead of alone and so far away. With a sigh, Molly slid into her jeans and pulled a sweatshirt out of her bottom drawer. There was nothing she could do for Prairie Lady — not yet.

As soon as she stepped outside the back door, the wind hit her. Wet and cold, it slid through her clothes to chill her to the bone. Shivering, she ran to the barn, where the wind probed around noisily, shaking the loose boards. But it was warm inside, and her blue mood lifted as the horses whickered their greetings, heads over their stall doors, waiting for their morning oats.

"Patience," she said, patting their noses on her way to the feed room. "After you eat, you just have to work, so don't be in such a hurry."

"Your wild horse is safe?" The low voice startled her so that she almost dropped the coffee can she used as a feed scoop.

"Dan," she gasped.

"I'm sorry," he said, "I thought you heard me."

"How did you know about the horse?" she asked, not really too surprised. She'd learned long ago that the prairie kept few secrets from the old Indian.

"The small halter was gone, some oats and salve. If it had been a hurt calf, you would have brought it home or told your father. Only a hurt wild horse would have to be a secret from everyone."

Molly smiled in answer to the warmth of his eyes. To someone who didn't know him, Dan might appear impassive and unfeeling, but his eyes held more expression than some people show in their whole face. "I hope she's all right, Dan, but I wish *you* could look at her."

"What's wrong with her?" Dan helped her feed the horses while she told him all about Lady.

"You did well, little maverick," he said. "She'll be safe enough in the canyon."

"But I can't hide her forever."

"It won't be easy," Dan agreed. "Your father is a good rancher and mostly he's right about the wild ones. It will take a lot to make him accept a mustang, especially for you to ride."

"That's the trouble. Lady's such a small, frightened thing. He'd scare her to death by just yelling at me. I don't know what I'm going to do, but I can't let her go, Dan. I love her."

"We'll think of something," Dan said. "But for now we'll have to be careful to keep the wild herd away from her when we run them today."

"Do you think we'll have any trouble?" Molly asked, grateful to have an ally.

"Who knows? Some herds are closer than families. They might have followed her up there from the creek or they might not. We'll just have to wait and see."

"What if they are up by the canyon?"

"When we know, we'll decide. Now I have work to do and so do you. I'll go see your Lady as soon as the wild ones are safely off the ranch. Okay?" His dark eyes smiled again reassuringly, then he left the barn.

Molly took her basket and braved the damp wind to the chicken house, searching for eggs among the nests while the hens scratched and complained in the yard. In a way, she was anxious for the wild horse roundup to be over. The filly would then be safe; and yet she would be sorry to have the herd chased off the range, where she could no longer watch them. She carried the eggs carefully to the house, whistling for Baron as she walked.

The old dog came to her slowly, his eager gait slowed by a limp. "Poor old dog,"

Molly said, pausing to pat his shaggy head, "the wet weather doesn't make you very frisky, does it?" The dog wagged his tail and licked her hand as he followed her inside.

"Looks like rain," her father said.

"Still going after the wild herd?" Molly asked.

"They eat just as much on rainy days. I'm getting fifty head of young cows from Murcheson next week, so I'll need all that grass."

Molly poured dry dog food into a dish for Baron, then took her place at the table. "Mom," she said, "is it okay if Baron stays inside today? He's limping again."

Her mother nodded. "Keep him in the laundry room though. He smells like a wet dog."

"Sometimes I think I should have bought you a puppy," her father said. "That dog is so old he's useless."

"It's just the damp weather, Daddy," Molly said. "He was fine yesterday."

"Maybe you took him too far on your hike," her mother said sharply.

Molly kept her eyes on her plate, wishing she could confide in her parents, but that would be risking the filly's life. They ate in silence for awhile. The only sound was that of Baron's dish sliding across the floor as he licked up the last crumb of food. When the dish was completely empty, he looked mournfully at the stairs to Molly's room, then when she shook her head, he padded out to his rug in the laundry. His sigh of resignation was clearly audible.

"Do you think you could spare Molly and me tomorrow, Jack?" her mother asked.

"I guess so. What's up?"

"I thought maybe we could do a little shopping." Her mother's words made Molly's skin prickle.

"Well, if it means spending money, I'm not sure I can spare you," her father said, winking at Molly.

"Just for material and patterns and things. We can use the long summer evenings to get some clothes made. After all, Molly's going to be in high school — she can't wear the same things she wore to school out here."

"All right, but don't forget I'm trying to start a blooded herd. Good cattle aren't cheap, and I've got to find a top bull before spring."

"Didn't Mr. Murcheson have any?" Molly asked, eager to turn the conversation away from high school or anything related to it.

"He had some beauties, but after I picked out the cows, I couldn't afford his price."

Molly swallowed a sigh, wishing, as she had so often, that they could raise horses instead of cattle. It would be really something to have herds of beautiful, purebred horses roaming their range. She had stopped listening to her parents' conversation and begun daydreaming of frisky foals and sturdy horses. Then a horse that was neither frisky nor sturdy popped into her mind and she wondered for the hundredth time if Prairie Lady was safe.

"Well, we'd better get to it," her father said, getting up. "It's a long ride to the fence line and if we have to hunt for that herd — "

"Do you want a lunch?" her mother asked.

He nodded. "You might fix a few sandwiches and coffee. It's going to be too wet for a fire."

"You'd both better get your heavy jackets out." Mrs. Rogers stacked the breakfast dishes and began making sandwiches.

Molly helped her mechanically, her mind on the wild herd and the cold filly up in the canyon.

They set out briskly, the wet wind smacking their faces and bringing the blood close to the surface. It hadn't rained yet, but the wind brought the smell of wet earth from the high country. The horses snorted and bounced a little, hating to go into the wind.

"I know how you feel, boy," Molly said, patting the neck of her cow pony.

"Well, Dan," her father said, "I guess we'll just follow you. Did Molly tell you where she saw them last?"

Dan nodded and turned his horse toward the creek. The big roan crowhopped and tried to rear, but Dan controlled him easily, riding with the peculiarly motionless style of a person who is truly part of his horse. Molly watched enviously. All Dan's teaching had made her a good rider, but she'd never achieved the perfect ease that he had.

"It happens, maverick," he always told her. "You can't learn it. Just wait and one day you'll have it." As she rode beside the two men, she could see that her father had never achieved it either.

They reached the hill above the creek so quickly that Molly hardly realized it. The plains were still and empty of life. Molly's heart sank. The herd had moved on, perhaps following the filly to her hiding place.

"Well, they aren't here," her father said.

"Where did you trail them to yesterday?"

"Well . . . a . . . they went north a little, I think," Molly answered miserably.

Her father's eyes searched her face as though he sensed that something was troubling her. But he said nothing, and in a moment Dan reined his roan around and rode off down the hill. Twice he stopped and dismounted to study the apparently trackless prairie. The trail he was following seemed to lead inevitably toward the box-canyon corral.

The horses were content to lope slowly over the wet grass, and stopped willingly whenever the riders reined in. Molly nudged her horse up beside her father. "Where will we drive them through?" she asked. "I mean, is the break, where they came in, still open?"

"Yes, we widened it so they'd have plenty of room to go through. I don't want to tangle any of them in the wire. It's all set to restring, so it won't take very long

— if we ever locate that herd."

"It's this side of the creek, isn't it?" Molly asked, her eyes searching ahead for the horses.

"Yes. If Dan's on the right trail, it won't be too hard to drive them that far."

Ahead of them, Dan appeared, signaling them to join him. Molly's heartbeat quickened. They were almost at the canyon; the herd must have followed the filly. Dan's eyes met hers. "The herd is just over the next rise," he said.

"How big is it?" her father asked.

"About twenty head and maybe a dozen foals. They're spread out, so I think it might be easier to come in from three sides and get them started in the right direction." Dan didn't look her way again, but Molly understood his plan.

"I'll go ahead," she said, "and ride down on them."

"You'll be pretty close to the old box canyon," her father said. "Maybe I'd better go that way. Those rocks will be slippery."

"Her horse isn't shod," Dan remarked. "He'll do better on the rocks than yours."

"I guess you're right. I'll go south and you take the center, Dan. Let's go, Molly."

Rain began pelting down as she and

her father rode off in opposite directions, leaving Dan to wait till they were in position. Molly buttoned the top of her jacket and pulled her father's old rain cap farther down over her eyes. She rode slowly and carefully, the loose shale was slick and she didn't want to scare the herd until Dan and her father were ready. She was halfway down the slope when her father came into view on the far side.

From her vantage point, she could see the herd grazing just beyond the corral. When her father appeared, the stallion snorted a warning and, to Molly's horror, began gathering his mares and heading them right into the canyon entrance.

Forgetting the slippery shale and everything else but the filly, Molly clapped her heels into her horse and began whooping and waving her arm. At first she thought the stallion hadn't seen her, but slowly he began cutting back out of the canyon toward the open country. Over the slither and rattle of her horse's hooves and the rush of the wind she heard the filly's frantic whinny, but there was no time to check on her. It took all of Molly's concentration to guide her horse over the slippery rocks,

49

and onto the grassy plains below.

Dan lifted his hand in a quick salute as he thundered by to join in the chase. Ahead, her father had turned the horses to the northwest and was riding beside the herd. Dan took up a similar post on the opposite side, and Molly eased her straining horse in behind the herd.

Gradually they slowed their horses from the headlong gallop to a steady, easy lope. The wild horses slowed too, keeping an even distance between themselves and the riders. Molly watched the wet, plunging horses ahead of her, almost hypnotized by their rhythmic pace and numbed with relief at Lady's close call. It wasn't till the wild herd split around the fence posts and then rejoined like a stream on the open prairie of the reservation that she lost her numbness.

The riders stopped together at the fence line, watching until the horses disappeared behind the gray curtain of rain and distance. Molly sighed, suddenly very tired, really feeling the wet and cold for the first time. She looked up at the sky, wondering what time it was, but the sun wasn't even a blur behind the clouds. The men slid off their heaving horses and Molly joined them.

"We'll put the wire up, Molly," her father said. "You can walk the horses a little. They've had a hard run, and I don't want them to get cold and stiff just standing around."

Molly took the reins obediently. The horses plodded behind her, stopping occasionally to munch off a mouthful of grass. She led them away from the fence until their breathing was normal and their wet hides no longer steamed in the cold wind. Then she turned back. When she reached the men, they were just finishing the last strand of wire.

"We might as well eat the sandwiches Annie made," her father said, digging in his saddlebags. "It's a long ride back."

"It sure turned out to be an awful day," Molly said, realizing that she was hungry, but finding the cold sandwich rather unappetizing.

"At least we didn't have to hunt for the herd half the day," her father said. "Thanks, Dan."

"Sure, Jack," Dan said. "Glad it was so easy."

"By the way, Molly," her father said, turning to face her, "that was a hare-brained stunt you pulled on the hill. One misstep on that shale and you'd have been killed. You know better than that."

"I'm sorry, Daddy." Molly kept her head down. "I guess when I saw that the horses were spooking, I just forgot everything else."

"I thought they were farther away, or I wouldn't have broken cover that way," her father explained. "But we could have run them back out of that old corral, you know."

"I just didn't think," Molly said, remembering her fears for the filly and how close her father had come to discovering her secret. She would have liked to ride home by way of the canyon, but knew it was out of the question. For today, at least, Prairie Lady was on her own.

"Well," her father said, getting up and shaking the rain from his hat, "we might as well head back. The ranch isn't getting any closer to us."

This time they rode slowly, close together but not talking. The wind whipped the rain against their backs, driving it under their hats to trickle coldly down their necks. The horses needed no urging or guiding. They were headed for the barn and their oats, and the rain whipped them along too.

It was close to four when they reached the ranch house. The wind was blowing harder, howling around the buildings. The rain had stopped and the clouds were being ripped apart by the wind. The sun broke through just as they led their horses into the barn.

"Now it clears up!" Molly said, hooking her stirrup on the horn and loosening the latigo strap to unsaddle.

"I'm glad we're through," her father said. "The wind is worse than the rain . . . blow you right off your horse."

Molly was glad that the wind had replaced the rain. Though it nearly took her breath away, she knew that Lady would be protected from the wind in the sheltered box canyon, and the last rays of the sun would dry her. The sky was a bright, new-washed blue. As the clouds disappeared over the eastern horizon, Molly sighed and went inside to receive Baron's enthusiastic welcome.

From the laundry, she overheard her

father saying, "I hope that's the last we see of the mustangs. They're sure a scrubby lot — not one I'd waste my time or feed on. We ought to get rid of all of them. They're just a nuisance."

Chapter 6

The next morning summer returned,
warm and sunny. The wind had dropped
during the night to a soft breeze. Molly
filled a bag with oats for Lady, after she
had done her chores, then hurried back
to the house, eager to eat breakfast and
be on her way to the canyon and her filly.

She waited until she was almost through
eating to ask, "Could I take one of the
horses for an hour or so this morning,
Daddy?"

"I suppose so," he said. "Where are you
planning to go?" He looked at her curiously, for this was an unusual request.

"Oh, I just thought I'd make sure we

got all the horses yesterday." It was a dangerous statement, but Molly could think of no other, and an outright lie to her parents came very hard.

"I'm sure we did. The stallion wouldn't let his herd split up. Why — do you think there were more? Did you notice some missing yesterday?"

She knew that she'd made a mistake and forced herself to smile.

"No, all the horses I saw in his herd were with him yesterday. I just thought it would be a good excuse for a ride. It's a beautiful day."

"Oh, no, you don't," her mother broke in. "You aren't slipping away today. You can help me with the wash, then we're going into town."

Molly swallowed her protests. She didn't want to press too hard and make her parents suspicious. "I'd forgotten," she said, all her enthusiasm gone. "I suppose the shopping won't wait?" It was half hope, half question.

"You're hopeless," her mother said, laughing fondly.

"If we're going into town," Molly said, "I'd better check with Dan and see if he wants me to get anything for him."

Her mother nodded, then said, "Tell him I'm going to fry some of the fish he brought back from his fishing trip tonight, and ask him to come to supper. He must be getting tired of his own cooking again."

"Yes, ma'am." Molly slipped out quickly, ran around behind the barn and down the well-worn path to Dan's cabin. He was sitting out in front, patiently teaching an orphaned calf to drink milk from a bucket. Molly stopped short, then began a slow approach so as not to scare the calf, whose brown eyes rolled her way nervously.

"He's a shy one," Dan said. "It's been a cruel world for him."

"I didn't know you had him," Molly said. "Where's his mother?"

"She was caught in a rockslide near the river. I found him when I was coming back from fishing."

Molly sat down — close enough so that the calf could watch her, but far enough away so that she wouldn't frighten him. Dan dipped his fingers in the milk again, holding them lower in the pail, trying to entice the calf to drink without sucking.

"Want me to get one of the bottles?" Molly asked.

"I have the one I used yesterday, but I don't think he'll need it. He's getting the idea pretty good now." The calf sucked noisily, choked on the milk, and nearly upset the pail. Dan soothed him and began again, infinitely patient.

"Who's that one for?" Molly asked.

"My grandson Bob, I think. He's old enough to learn to care for a good calf."

Molly smiled. For as long as she could remember, her father had given Dan all the orphaned calves he found. Most ranchers were too busy to take care of orphans and gave them a quick death, but Dan made time, and his widely scattered family always had need of another calf. Her father called the calves Dan's bonus for staying on the ranch instead of moving in with one of his children after his wife died. Molly suspected that her father really considered them a way of making up for not being able to pay Dan what he was really worth.

"What can I do for you?" Dan asked, sitting back with a pleased sigh. The calf was drinking alone now, snorting and choking a little, but he'd learned to keep trying and that was the most important lesson.

"I came to ask a favor," Molly said.

"For the wild one?"

Molly nodded. "I have to go into town with Mom, and I just want to know if she's all right. I mean, if she fell on her bad side and couldn't get up again, she could die out there alone."

"This afternoon I'll ride by the canyon and leave some oats for her. I want to see this gift from the wild herd."

"Thanks, Dan. Is there anything you need from town?"

"What could I want from town?" His eyes were warm. He smacked the calf lightly on the rump, sending it bouncing for the pen. "You go on and meet your new classmates," he said.

"We're just going shopping," Molly said, though she knew that wasn't her mother's only reason for taking her into town.

"Don't fight it," Dan said. "Even little mavericks have to grow up and take their place in the herd."

"My place is here," Molly said defiantly.

"This is one of them," Dan agreed.

"Molly! Molly!" Her mother's call interrupted their conversation.

"Coming," Molly answered, then turned

back to Dan. "Mom said she'd fry some of the fish you caught in Hidden Valley, so come up for supper."

Dan nodded, reaching into his pocket for some bits of corn bread to feed the ground squirrels that were venturing out from under his rough wood porch. Molly left feeling lonelier, as though his acceptance of her growing up had robbed her of an ally.

The main street of Medford was crowded with cars, many of them bearing out-of-state license plates. This was tourist season, and the visitors were heading for the mountains and lakes west of the town. Molly looked around, feeling curious and yet shy among all these people. "Where do they all come from?" her mother asked, a smile brightening her whole face. "I'll never find a parking place with this crowd."

"We could come back some other day," Molly suggested hopefully. The winter-empty streets were bad enough, but the throngs of relaxed, laughing people made her feel her own loneliness more acutely. She would never fit in, she was sure.

"Go home?" Her mother laughed. "You don't think I drove forty miles just to look at people and run? Oh, Molly, you are a silly one."

"There sure are a lot more tourists this year," Molly said.

"That's what makes it fun," her mother said. "Sometimes I get so lonesome at the ranch, I think I'll die if I don't see a new face or listen to something besides ranch talk."

"I never do," Molly said quietly. It was true; she wasn't lonesome the same way her mother was. She missed Linda, but just being with people wouldn't make her feel less alone.

"I wish you did." Her mother backed the car into a narrow space, then bounced out of the car, urging Molly to join her.

The shopping turned out to be less painful than Molly had expected. They selected six patterns and the wool, corduroy, and dark cotton materials to make them. It took a few hours and visits to all three of the Medford stores that sold fabrics, but finally they were heading back for the car, loaded with packages.

"How about a soda before we go to the grocery store?" her mother asked as they put the bundles into the car.

"Fine," Molly said, though she really

wasn't too eager to visit the drugstore. Once inside, however, her eyes were drawn immediately to a huge poster tacked to the back wall beside the blaring jukebox. "Excuse me a minute, Mom," she said.

"Go ahead, dear, I want to look around anyway."

Molly threaded her way up the aisle and between the booths crowded with teenagers. The poster showed a huge black horse painted in the traditional quarter-horse sliding stop. Big red letters above him spelled "GYMKHANA." She was reading the list of events when the music stopped.

"How do you like the art work?" a boy's voice asked.

Molly turned slowly, acutely conscious of the eyes that might be watching her. "It's great," she said, softly. "Did you do it?"

"Sure did. That's my quarter horse, Pecos. I'm Paul Bradford."

Molly introduced herself. "He's a beauty," she said, trying to force her face into a friendly smile, but her shyness made it feel artificial.

"You have a horse?" he asked, not seeming to notice her shyness at all.

"Yes, a filly." Molly's nervousness eased

a little as she thought of Prairie Lady. "She's not like him, though. She's a mustang."

"Hey, that's great. Are you going to enter her in any of the gymkhana events?"

"I'm not sure I can. She's not broken in yet." Molly almost forget her shyness as she talked about Lady.

"You've got till the middle of August," Paul said. "It really isn't so much the competition as it is just the fun. I've ridden in it almost every year I can remember."

"What are you trying to do, Paul, scare up some more competition for me?" a girl's voice asked.

Molly turned and immediately felt her shyness returning. The girl had long blond hair and expensive clothes. She looked just like a magazine illustration to Molly, and made her feel self-conscious in her worn jeans and old shirt. Though she guessed that they were the same age, the girl made Molly feel an awkward ten.

"Are you from around here?" the girl purred, her blue eyes cold.

"I . . . a . . . live on a ranch up by Pine Creek," Molly stammered.

"Oh." The word seemed to sum up her

entire opinion of Molly and anyone else who lived on a ranch.

"She's got a mustang filly she's going to break," Paul explained. Molly turned back to him gratefully, but before she could say anything, the girl led Paul away.

"See you around, Molly," Paul said. "Good luck with your filly."

Molly felt abandoned. She wasn't sure how the girl had done it, but somehow Molly was far lonelier than she had been before she talked to Paul.

"Don't mind Robin," another girl's voice said. "She's got a superiority complex and she has to feed it."

Molly looked around and met a pair of understanding brown eyes. "I don't mind," she said, wishing that it were true.

"I'm Ginger Kahn. Are you new in town?"

"Molly Rogers. I was born here. I live forty miles north of town. We don't get in much." Molly waited for the look she'd seen in Robin's face, but it didn't come.

"Gee, I'd die if I couldn't come down here every day. What do you do out there?"

Molly relaxed a little, thinking of Dan and the filly, her walks with Baron, and

trailing the wild herd. She started to tell
Ginger about the filly, but before she had
a chance, another boy came up and tapped
Ginger on the shoulder. Ginger shrugged,
grinned at Molly, and went with him. Molly
stood alone by the jukebox, feeling left out
and yet afraid to be asked to join in.

Robin and Ginger seemed so at home
here. Molly sighed, then caught sight of her
mother, obviously looking for her. Molly
hesitated a moment, wanting to talk to
Ginger again, then decided that it wouldn't
do any good. She kept her head down as
she passed the crowded booths, feeling prying
eyes through the high fence of her own
shyness. Wanting to fit in wasn't enough,
she knew. And it wouldn't be easy; Robin
had made that clear.

"Well, did you meet some of your future
classmates?" her mother asked as they
walked back along the counter, looking for
two vacant stools.

"A few of them. I was looking at the
poster."

"Are they nice?" The enthusiasm in her
mother's voice made Molly feel even worse.

"Fine, Mom, just great." They found two
stools and Molly sank down gratefully.

"What did you buy?" she asked, hoping to change the subject.

"Not much. I just like to look at all the cosmetics and jewelry. Do you want a soda?"

Once in the grocery store and twice on their way home, her mother asked her about the boys and girls in the drugstore. Each time Molly tried to change the subject, not wanting to disappoint her mother with the truth. But by the time they reached the ranch, she had told her how nice Paul and Ginger had been. By ignoring her encounter with Robin, it didn't sound too bad. Her mother seemed pleased and finally left Molly to sort the whole thing out for herself.

It was true that Paul and Ginger had been friendly, but it was in a casual way, as though they were used to meeting new people. Paul had been interested in the filly, but that was the only interest she'd shared with any of them. Most of all, she thought of Robin's snub. It was cruel, and what made it worse was the fact that she had no idea why Robin didn't like her.

Molly was still mulling it over as she helped her mother fix supper. It wasn't until Dan came in that she thought again of the filly. But with her parents present, she couldn't ask Dan how Lady was, and the meal seemed to drag on forever. Her mother made it worse by telling Dan and her father about her "friends" in the drugstore, and the way she told it made Molly blush with shame. She was sorry now that she hadn't told her mother about Robin. Her mother's disappointment would have been easier to live with than this false success story. She felt relieved when dinner was over and the dishes were done.

Dan was waiting for her at the corral, leaning on the rail and scratching the roan's ears. "Been expecting you, Molly," he said, not even turning to be sure who it was.

"I came as soon as I could." Molly leaned beside him. "How's Lady?"

"Near as I could see, she seems to be healing okay. Still limps, but not too much. She's got plenty of grass for another two or three weeks, and the spring is keeping the pool full of water."

"How about her neck — are the welts healed?" Relief made the hurt and confusion of the afternoon seem far away.

"I didn't get close enough to see, and I didn't think roping her would be a good idea. I left the oats by the spring and she was eating them when I left."

Suddenly the implication of his words began to seep through to Molly and she turned to look at him. "You mean she ran from you?"

"She's a mustang, Molly, and I was a stranger to her."

"But she was so gentle down by the creek, and she never was afraid of me."

"She was almost dead when you found her. Now she's nearly well. You go up there tomorrow. Don't give her a chance to forget you."

"Do you think she would?" Molly asked, horrified at the idea.

"There's no way to tell. She's run wild all her life and the only humans she's been around hurt and scared her. She's young, so you've got a better-than-average chance of taming her, but it takes time and a lot of just being with her."

"But . . ." It didn't seem fair, Molly thought, remembering how she'd worried and cared about Lady. She'd been so sure that loving the filly was all it took. Now Dan made it seem so much more difficult.

"Don't fret about it till you go up and see for yourself. You can take Jackrabbit tomorrow. Your Dad's loaning me the pickup to deliver the calf to my grandson, so I won't need the horse."

"Thanks, Dan," Molly said, her heart heavy. "Good night."

"Don't fight the world, maverick. Take it as it comes and do what you can — you'll get further, easier."

She left him standing at the rail, still rubbing his horse's neck and studying the darkening sky. His words were wise, she knew, but they didn't tell her how to stop caring about the things she was fighting for. The filly, her way of life here on the ranch, her dreams of Lady's future — they meant too much to just give up. Molly brushed a tear away. She had to make them come true, no matter how difficult the fight.

Chapter 7

In the morning Molly rushed through her chores and in to breakfast. As she ate, she waited for her father's inevitable question. It came just as she began stacking her dishes to carry to the sink.

"Where are you going today?" he asked.

"Dan said he didn't need Jackrabbit today, so I thought I'd go for a ride." She paused and forced a smile. "Did you have something you wanted me to do?"

"As a matter of fact, I was going to suggest you take one of the horses and ride the north fence line. Murcheson is delivering the cows tomorrow, and I don't want to take any chances with them when I turn them out."

"Okay, sure, Daddy," she said, trying to keep the disappointment out of her voice. "I'll take a lunch with me then."

"While you're at it, make two," he said. "I'm riding the south fence."

It could have been worse, Molly decided, as she made the sandwiches. At least, the box-canyon corral was near the northern fence line. If she rode quickly, she'd have time to stop and see the filly. It wasn't exactly the way she'd planned it, but she would be alone and in no danger of being discovered — that was the most important thing.

When she went out, Baron came bounding up to her, tail wagging. "No, Baron," she said, knowing that the trip would be much too hard for the old dog. "You stay," she ordered. "Next time you can go." The dog's tail drooped as he walked to the laundry room door. The look of sadness about him made Molly feel guilty, and she hurried on.

In the barn, she added her lunch to the already bulging saddle bags, then led Dan's tall roan out to the corral. By the time her father led his horse out of the barn, she was wishing that she'd taken his suggestion and used one of their horses instead of Jackrabbit.

The big red horse was much taller than most cow ponies, but he handled his long legs with the agility of a cat. Dan had won roping and cow-cutting contests from his back; in fact, Molly knew that the down payment for Dan's youngest son's ranch had come from Jackrabbit's winnings.

Molly gritted her teeth as Jackrabbit reared and plunged forward, kicking out the extra-long hind legs that had given him his name. She knew from experience that it would take two or three more playful bucks before the big horse was ready to work. As Dan said, he wasn't mean, he just didn't intend to be ridden by an amateur.

When he finally stopped and nuzzled her knee, admitting defeat, Molly rode back to where her father sat on his horse, watching.

"I'll never understand you," he said, shaking his head. "I've got three good, gentle saddle horses and you take out that ornery jughead."

"He's the best cow horse on the ranch," Molly said. "You admitted that when he won the State cow-cutting championship."

"Sure, but you're not going after cattle and he always puts up a fight before he lets anyone ride him."

"He's independent," Molly said, suddenly glad she was riding the roan. "He *lets* people ride him instead of doing it because he has to."

Her father wasn't impressed. "That's what comes of trying to train a stupid mustang. You be careful now, and I want you back by supper." He turned his horse away before she could argue further about the value of wild horses.

Molly reined the big roan around and they set off for the northeast corner of the ranch at his ground-eating lope. Clumsy though he might look, his easy lope and long-legged running walk made him the smoothest riding horse she'd ever been on, and he was almost tireless.

"Jackrabbit," she said, rubbing his satiny shoulder, "I think you're the best advertisement I've seen for using wild horses. Daddy just doesn't understand you." The horse snorted softly, and his ears turned back to listen as she told him about the filly and the wild herd.

Some people hated riding fence lines, but

Molly honestly enjoyed it. It was easier for her to talk to horses than to most humans. When she was little, her father had taken her around the entire ranch in a jeep. Horses were slower, but the beauty of the prairie made the time pass easily.

A jackrabbit shot up, almost under the roan's hooves, and bounced across the grass to disappear into a small draw. The horse shied at his namesake, nearly unseating Molly. She laughed, wishing that Baron were younger and could come on these long rides. He was growing old and she was growing up and the filly . . . was she growing wild again? Molly sighed, wishing that life could go on forever at the happy points, not letting time change everything.

It was nearly noon when she turned Jackrabbit south, away from the fence line, to head for the box canyon. The sun was hot now, and even the indestructible roan was beginning to get damp patches of sweat on his back and shoulders. Molly patted him, feeling a little guilty for pushing him so hard. "I'll leave early, Jackrabbit," she promised, "and we'll take it easy the rest of the way."

The canyon was cooler. By the time they reached the fence of the small corral and Jackrabbit was unsaddled, the sweat patches were dry and hard. As she worked around the roan, Molly watched for Lady, knowing that she must have heard their approach. The corral was small, but the uneven canyon walls and the trees around the spring offered many hiding places.

Carrying only a lead rope and the saddlebags, Molly untied the gate and led the roan inside. She knotted the reins loosely, high around his neck so they wouldn't drag on the ground under his feet, then turned him loose. Almost immediately the filly appeared from behind the rocks near the spring. She approached the big horse slowly, head high, limping hardly at all.

Molly was astonished at what the two days had done for her horse. The gaunt line of ribs and pointed hip bones had vanished completely; the lusterless brown of her coat had become the red-gold sheen of chestnut; and her mane and tail rippled a darker red-brown as she walked. About three feet from where the roan was drinking, Lady stopped and whickered to him. Jackrabbit looked at her, snorted, then turned his attention back to the pool and the lush grass beside it.

"Hello, little Lady," Molly said, dropping the saddlebags and rope. She came forward carrying only a few molasses cubes. "How's my girl? Remember me?" She walked very slowly.

Lady stood her ground, ears twitching forward and back with indecision. Molly kept talking, holding a cube out for her to see and smell. One thing was clear, the filly hadn't forgotten her. But how many of her wild instincts had returned was quite another question. She definitely wasn't the same horse Molly had turned loose only two days before.

When she reached the filly, time seemed to stand still. Lady sniffed her fingers delicately, tickling them with her warm breath. When she took the cube, Molly reached up to touch her neck. The filly tried to move away, but Molly caught the halter, forcing Lady to endure the petting and rubbing until she relaxed and began to enjoy it.

Finally Molly put her arm around the filly's neck and gently guided her over to the saddlebags. Once there, she poured out two piles of oats, a small one for Jackrabbit and a larger one for the filly. Then she sat down under a tree a few feet away and ate her own lunch.

When the horses had finished eating, Molly got up and went over to the filly. This time she had no trouble approaching Lady. The filly nuzzled her with obvious love. Molly rubbed her for a moment, then reached into the grass for the lead rope. She wanted to tie Lady while she examined her injured fetlock to see how the rope burn and sprain were healing.

Without warning the filly reared up and broke away. Her shoulder hit Molly, knocking her to the ground. The girl lay still for a few seconds, fighting the pain of gasping for breath. After a moment the pain eased and she sat up, breathing normally.

The filly was standing under the trees again, watching, her ears flipping questioningly. Molly got up slowly, surprised to find that she really wasn't hurt. The blow from the filly's shoulder had knocked the breath out of her, nothing more. Feeling a little better, she looked around to see what could have frightened the filly.

The ground where they'd been standing was like any other spot in the corral, no

small animal or bird had come out to startle
her. Jackrabbit was grazing peacefully by
the pond. Frowning, Molly picked up the
rope and dug a cube out of her pocket, then
started after Lady again.

This time she couldn't get close to her.
For almost an hour she stalked the filly
around and around the corral. Lady's slight
limp didn't slow her a bit; she dodged
among the trees and around the pool in a
way that showed clearly the teachings of
her life with the wild herd.

Molly's hopes dropped with every passing moment. What had she done wrong?
she stopped to ask herself. The filly had
been shy at first, but not like this. She'd
been easy to catch, even friendly. When
she'd reached for the rope to . . . Molly
looked at the rope in her hand, everything
suddenly began to make sense to her.

Lady had been roped and badly frightened before she had come onto the ranch
with the herd. That same rope had nearly
cost her her life in the clearing. The pain
in her leg had come from the rope, and
Molly herself had undoubtedly hurt her
with the rope when she turned her over.
Lady had been too sick and weak to even shy

from it then, but now that she was strong again the memory of her pain and fright was clear.

Molly tucked the rope under the saddlebags and, armed only with molasses cubes, began following the filly. It took a little longer than it had when she first arrived, but before long she was stroking the silky hide and being nuzzled.

"Lady," Molly said, "I'm sorry you're afraid, but you can't go on running from ropes. If you're going to be my horse, you'll have to get used to them. They won't hurt you, really."

The filly stood quietly while Molly walked around and around her, touching her sides, her back, running a hand down her legs and generally getting her used to the touch of human hands. Lady didn't even object when Molly examined the fetlock. The swelling was completely gone and the rope burns around it were healing over well.

"Now, Lady," Molly said, when she was sure the filly was calm, "it's time for your first lesson. I can't take you home till you learn to lead like a proper horse, so let's see if I can change your mind about ropes."

The filly followed her to the saddlebags

willingly enough and stood quietly while
Molly dug out another molasses cube. She
moved the bags a little, exposing the rope.
The filly eyed it, but stood her ground,
eating the cube and letting Molly rub her.
Using her foot, Molly shoved the bag further off the rope, holding Lady when she
tried to run away. She petted the filly and
talked to her until she began to lose interest
in the rope.

It took a long time to get the rope completely uncovered, and longer still to coax
the filly a step closer to it. Finally, however, Lady put her head down and sniffed it
cautiously. That called for more praise and
petting. Then, deciding that she'd gone far
enough for the first lesson, Molly walked
back toward the spring.

Lady followed without a rope, trotting
along behind her almost as Baron did. She
stood patiently while Molly twisted wild
flowers in her mane, and then ran through
the tall grass in a rather rough game of
tag. Lady would nudge Molly, then run a
few yards away, obviously inviting Molly
to chase her. When she did, Lady ran on,
always staying just out of reach. Whenever
Molly gave up and turned away, Lady

would come up, nudge her again, and the game would start all over.

They played for a long time. Molly marvelled at the intelligence of the filly and her willingness to play like a puppy. Though she'd been around saddle horses all her life, Molly found Lady different from any horse she'd ever known. Finally, tired and hot, Molly sank down under a tree to rest. The filly came over and stood beside her, her eyes reflecting her complete love and trust of this one human. Molly was happier than she'd ever been.

A sharp whinny awakened her. For a moment she wasn't sure where she was, then she remembered and scrambled to her feet. The filly was no longer beside her, but another whinny helped Molly locate her. She was standing at the foot of the back canyon wall, looking up longingly. Molly followed her gaze, but could see nothing.

"Hey, Lady," she called, but the filly didn't turn.

Molly looked around, suddenly aware of the lengthening shadows; it was late afternoon, nearly five, she judged. Horrified, she thought of her father's words this morning.

"I want you back in time for supper," he'd said and she still had almost half the fence to check.

The roan was cropping grass contentedly, but he didn't object when she led him to the fence and hurriedly cinched on the saddle. As soon as she finished gathering her belongings, she took the few remaining molasses cubes and went to bid the filly good-bye.

Lady hardly seemed to notice her, and she wasn't interested in the cubes. After a few minutes Molly sighed, set the cubes down, and walked back to Jackrabbit. The closeness she'd felt earlier and the wonder of playing with the filly seemed like a dream now. She had been shut out — something wild and free outside the canyon was calling to the filly and Lady could hear nothing else.

Chapter 8

Molly realized that she wouldn't have time to finish the fence inspection. As it was, she'd barely make it home in time for supper. Still, she took a few precious moments to ride up to the top of the canyon and lope the roan across the plateau to its highest point. From there she could see a great deal of the fence line. As far as she could see, it was an unbroken line of posts, but at this distance it was impossible to tell if the wire was still strung between them.

Sighing, she started to turn Jackrabbit when a movement beyond the fence caught her eye. A ringing whinny came from the canyon below, and was answered from the plains — the wild horse herd was again seeking its missing member. They were on the reservation side of the fence, but they seemed to know where the filly was.

Jackrabbit began to tremble and fight the bit and Molly had a hard time turning him away from the fence. When she pushed him into a lope, he looked back longingly and once even added his bugling to the lonesome filly's whinnies.

Eight years Dan had had him, eight years of riding and training, barns and oats, love and care, and still Jackrabbit remembered the free life and called to the wild herd. Molly couldn't help wondering if her father had been right. No matter how friendly the filly had been, when the wild herd appeared, she'd left Molly and forgotten everything but her desire to join them.

For a moment Molly slowed Jackrabbit and considered setting Lady free. Her leg was well enough now, and it would be easy to let her out through one of the gates in the fence line . . . then Molly remembered how the filly had played with her, the touch of the velvet nose against her hand, and she kicked Jackrabbit into a gallop, heading home.

It was late when she reached the ranch buildings, but her father was still in the barn when she led Jackrabbit in. As soon as she saw him, she thought guiltily of the fence she'd failed to inspect. What if it was down farther on? But if it had been, she reasoned, the wild herd would have come in, so it must be all right.

"Hi, Daddy," she said and began unsaddling.

"About time you got in. That horse give you any trouble?" His voice was gruff, but she knew it was because he'd worried. If only she hadn't fallen asleep. "No, he's an angel to ride, really. He makes all his fuss here at the barn."

"How's the north fence?"

"I didn't find any breaks. Did you?" That wasn't exactly a lie, she told herself, hating the fact that she still had to compromise with the truth to protect the filly. If only her father could understand how she felt about Lady — she sighed wearily.

"Not a one. We had a good winter, I guess. I'll call Murcheson tonight and see if he can deliver the cows tomorrow."

"So soon?" Molly asked, then wished she hadn't.

"Why not? The pasture's ready, isn't it?"

"I just thought you said it would be a week." Molly carried her saddle and bridle into the feed room and scooped up a generous pail of oats for Jackrabbit.

"The deal went through easier than I thought it would. I can sign the papers for the new cows and get rid of our old herd at the same time. There's no reason to wait, is there? I'll go to the bank and do it tomorrow."

"Who's going to take our herd?" Molly asked, more for something to say than because she cared about the cattle.

"Jenner-Simmons. They'll pick them up in a couple of weeks. They'll take some for beef and sell the rest to new ranchers for herds. They gave me a pretty good price — better than I could get on my own, I think."

"That's good," Molly said, thinking mainly that she'd have time to ride the rest of the fence in the morning while her father was in town signing the papers.

"I'd like you to come with me," he said, shattering that plan.

"But, Daddy . . ." Molly protested.

"Your mother's birthday is in a couple of weeks and I need some help with a present. You don't have anything else to do, do you?"

Molly thought sadly of the filly and the fence, neither of which she could mention and both of which she wanted very much to see about. "No, nothing important," she said. "I'd like to get Mom's present then too."

"We'll go early so I can be back before Murcheson comes. He'll need help unloading and I want to check the cows over before I turn them out."

"Any calves?" Molly asked, thinking of the little orphan that Dan had been feeding.

"Just a few. These are all young stock. Most of them will be having their first calves next spring."

"I'll go up and help Mom with dinner," Molly said, giving Jackrabbit a final pat.

"Sure, go ahead. I'll be along in a few minutes."

Outside the sun was dropping heavily toward the mountains and Molly felt very weary. The blow she'd taken from the filly's shoulder made her bones ache, and the memory of Lady's heartbroken calls to the wild herd hurt too — more than anything.

Morning came too soon and with it the trip to town. When she was younger, Molly loved going anywhere with her father, but now the pressure from her parents to make friends in town took away all the pleasure. She put on a dress, at her mother's insistence, sure now that her father was planning a trip to the drugstore and not knowing how she could avoid it.

The streets were uncrowded when her father parked near the bank, but by the time all the papers were signed, and they came out into the sunshine again, the sidewalks were crowded. Molly walked at her father's side, feeling uncomfortable in a dress.

"How about something cold before we start shopping?" her father asked. "Signing papers and writing checks is thirsty work."

"Sure, Daddy, whatever you want," Molly said, wishing fervently that she were back on the ranch. She was afraid to see the crowd in the drugstore again, afraid of having her father see that she really wasn't making friends, not the way her mother thought she was.

To her surprise the drugstore was nearly empty. There wasn't a young person in sight, and even the jukebox was still. Molly relaxed a little. Then, sensing her father's disappointment, she said, "See that poster by the jukebox? I was talking to the boy who drew it. That's his own horse. He's going to ride him in the gymkhana."

"Do many boys and girls in town enter?" her father asked.

"I think so. It's a pretty big event here." Molly felt a cold finger of doubt at the thoughtful look she saw in her father's eyes.

"Maybe you should enter some of the events," he said, just as she'd feared he would.

"I don't know what they are," Molly said hastily. "I mean, I've never even heard of most of them."

"Like what?"

"Oh, the potato race, the barrel-and-stake, and pole-bending, and I forget what all. The only one I recognized was the barrel race and that's 'cause we saw one at last year's rodeo."

Her father began explaining some of the

events, and Molly asked lots of questions, hoping that he would forget about her entering the competition. By the time their sodas were gone, he was back talking about the herd of cattle and she could relax.

The shopping was easy — a fluffy robe from her father and matching slippers from Molly. As soon as the gifts were wrapped and safely hidden in the trunk of the car, Molly and her father started home.

Right after lunch, the prairie quiet was broken by the clatter and roar of a huge cattle truck bumping its way over the hill and turning into the ranch yard. By the time Molly and her father reached the corral, Mr. Murcheson had backed the truck into position beside the corral gate and was ready to move the ramp into place.

Molly leaned on the sun-warmed wood and stared at the closely packed cattle. She could see why her father was willing to go into debt to buy them. Though they were no bigger than the half-breed range cattle he had been raising, the rich red-and-white coats covered square, deep-chested bodies. They all stood patiently while the men rigged the ramp and took down the truck gate.

"Open the corral gate, Molly," her father called.

Molly ran to obey, and when she turned back, the first cow was standing uncertainly at the top of the ramp. Her father went up and gently urged the cow to take the first step. The others followed easily, coming down in two's and three's, a few with knobby calves clinging tightly to their sides.

Molly counted them as she watched the unloading. Fifty cows, all fat and perfect, hardly distinguishable except for the small differences in their white markings. Only seven had calves, four little bulls and three heifers. Molly held out her hand to the last calf, touching his warm, quivering side. Quick as a bird, he dashed away, and his mother turned reproachful eyes on Molly.

"I'm sorry," Molly said, patting the cow's soft shoulder. "I didn't mean to scare your baby. I wouldn't hurt him for anything, really I wouldn't."

The cow stood contentedly, unafraid, so different from the spooky range cattle Molly was used to. She scratched the cow for a moment, then closed the gate. Her father and Mr. Murcheson were talking, so

Molly walked around to the other side of the corral, where Dan was tying the three saddled horses.

"Looks like a good herd," Dan said, bending down to examine Jackrabbit's front hoof.

"They sure are," Molly agreed. "What's wrong with Jackrabbit?"

"Just a little rock, but I pried it out. You must have given him a good ride yesterday, he's sure quiet today."

Molly rubbed the red-gray muzzle and smiled. "He's a good horse, isn't he?"

"One of the best. And how's your filly? Did she remember you?"

"Oh, yes. She played like a puppy with me. But she's deathly afraid of ropes now — I guess because she was hurt so badly by one."

Dan nodded. "It takes time and patience, but if she likes you as much as you say, you can make her forget the bad times."

"Dan," Molly began, playing with Jackrabbit's mane to keep from looking into his too-knowing eyes, "I saw the wild herd yesterday — on the reservation. They were looking for the filly again."

"They will until she comes here and loses the wild scent forever."

"Jackrabbit wanted to go with them," Molly said, wondering if Dan would feel as hurt as she did. To her surprise, he laughed.

"The old fool," he said. "He's just dreaming. First blizzard he'd be here looking for oats and a warm stall. He's too wise to wish to be wild again, at least for very long."

The words soothed her doubts a little. "Are you sure, Dan?" she asked. "I mean, what about the filly?"

"Did Jackrabbit buck or fight you to go with the herd?"

Molly shook her head.

"The filly still has to learn, but someday she'll know that this life is better. Any horse will go with a wild herd if he gets a chance, it's their nature, but most of them are glad when their owners bring them back."

"I hope so," Molly said, thinking of the filly. "I really hope so."

Molly leaned on the corral, watching the men check over the cows, waiting for them to finish so she could help her father and Dan take them out to pasture. She tried to believe Dan's reassuring words, but it seemed so different for him and Jackrabbit. After all Jackrabbit had been a colt when Dan had caught him and Lady was a three-year-old, almost full-grown. She was still worrying when her father called to her to bring the horses over to the gate.

They took the herd along the creek, not hurrying them, but keeping them together and moving. "We'll have to check there every day for a week or so," her father said. "They've been pretty much pen-raised, and I want to be sure they'll stay in a herd in this strange pasture."

"I'd be glad to do it, Daddy," Molly said quickly. "I don't have anything else to do."

"Fine. It won't be much of a job, just come out and rough-count them, see that they're not too spread out."

Molly nodded, thinking how easy it would be to check the herd and then ride up to the box canyon and work with the filly. She didn't have much more time. The grass in the small corral wouldn't last forever, and when it was gone the filly would have to be moved.

Chapter 9

The next morning the wind was again snarling at the house, but Molly ignored it. She hurried through her chores and waited impatiently as her mother made pancakes for breakfast. As Molly ate, her mother asked, "How about working on your school clothes today?"

"I can't," Molly said quickly, "I have to check the new herd for Daddy."

"Well, that won't take all day, will it? You can go this morning and I'll have my work finished when you get back. That way, we'll have the whole afternoon."

"Okay. But I don't see why the hurry. This is only June."

"You'll be surprised how fast the summer will go. It'll be schooltime before you know it."

Molly smothered a shudder at the thought of high school and went on eating. She would go to the canyon, she decided, but she wouldn't be able to stay as long as she'd planned. There wouldn't be time for her to finish checking the fence, but that could wait until tomorrow. The new cows wouldn't be wandering far, she was sure.

When she whistled for Baron, he came out of the laundry room very slowly, limping badly. Molly knelt beside him, her fingers gently probing his front paw. She found nothing, though he whined whenever she touched the joint. Groaning under his weight, she carried him down to Dan's cabin, forgetting her hurry in her concern for her dog.

"It's just age, I think," Dan said when he'd finished examining the dog's paw. "Like rheumatism. Leave him home for a while and I think it'll heal itself. He could have strained or twisted his paw chasing rabbits."

Molly thanked Dan and took Baron back to the house, telling him regretfully to stay.

Her ride to check the herd would be lonelier without him, but she was glad there wasn't anything serious wrong with him.

Riding into the wind took most of the pleasure out of the trip, and she was glad when she located the herd. They were spread out a little, grazing peacefully while the calves slept in the warm grass.

A quick count told her that none had strayed, and she turned north, eager to see if Lady was safe and try to convince her that life with the wild herd really wasn't the best life. In her saddlebags she not only had oats and cubes, but two carrots and an apple to help Lady make up her mind.

When Molly reached the corral, she was happy to see that Lady was grazing calmly beside the pool. The horse she was riding whinnied a greeting, and Lady came over to touch noses with him while Molly unsaddled. Lady wasn't a bit shy, and nearly knocked Molly down with the friendliness of her greeting.

Molly poured out the oats for Lady, making a small pile for her riding horse as well. While they ate, she cautiously took a short rope from her saddlebag and tied it loosely around her waist. Then she made a quick inspection of the enclosure.

There was a new rockslide on the north wall, and Molly wondered if it might have been started by Lady in an attempt to get out to join the wild herd. The grass was still plentiful, but the look of lushness was gone; the filly was definitely eating it down. Molly couldn't tell how long it would last, but Dan's estimate of two or three weeks seemed close.

She was still studying the turf when a soft muzzle hit her between the shoulder blades. She turned and the filly raced away.

"So you want to play, do you?" Molly laughed and began the game, knowing that she was wasting valuable training time but unable to resist the filly's teasing. As they dodged through the trees and ran across the grass, Molly realized that Lady no longer had even a trace of her limp. She was filled out and sleek and looked as though she'd never been hurt or sick.

"Lady," she said, when the filly suddenly surrendered and stood still to be rubbed, "you really are a beauty. I underestimated you. Even Daddy will have to admit you're pretty."

Speaking of her father brought her other problems back to her. Still petting Lady and talking to her, she untied the rope from her waist and slipped it, unnoticed, up to the ring in the filly's halter. She had the first knot tied when the wind whipped the loose end against Lady's chest.

The change was instantaneous. Lady jerked back, half rearing. Molly held tight to the halter, still talking, trying to soothe the filly, but Lady didn't seem to hear. Her ears were tight against her head and the gentle eyes were now white-ringed with fear. She plunged forward.

Molly gritted her teeth and held on, trying to run to keep from falling. Her hands began to burn and the muscles in her arms felt as though they were being yanked loose. Tears of helpless fury burned in her eyes, blurring everything. Then her feet hit a rock, and with a last frantic wrench, her hold on the halter was broken. She sprawled heavily to the ground.

For a minute she was too dazed to move, then she wished she didn't have to. Lady didn't trust her. All their playing together and friendliness had meant nothing to her the moment the rope touched her. Slowly, painfully, Molly lifted her face from the grass and looked around. Lady was still running, the short rope streaming back to touch her on the neck and shoulders. Molly put her face down on her arms and gave in to her tears.

It had all come to nothing — saving Lady, loving her, trying to make her tame and gentle. It was a waste because she couldn't forget the terror she'd known at someone else's hands. She would have to be turned loose, Molly knew, for there was no place on a ranch for a horse that was as rope-shy as Lady. The fact that Molly understood why Lady was rope-shy made no difference. If the filly couldn't overcome her fear, she would be a danger to herself and to anyone who rode her.

And Molly's dreams of having a horse of her own, a horse who was a real friend and companion, faded. Her father would never know it, but he'd been right — a wild horse was useless. Jackrabbit was an accident, another example of Dan's special magic with animals. She'd been a fool to even hope, she told herself, trying hard not to go on loving the unhappy filly.

Suddenly warm velvet tickled Molly's cheek and a soft whicker was blown in her ear. She held her breath, afraid to believe. The velvety nose pushed harder, more demandingly. Molly rolled over and sat up.

The filly stood above her, dripping with the sweat of fear and violent running. White still showed in her eyes, but love was there too. She took a step closer to Molly, shuddering when the rope touched her leg, but no longer fleeing from it. Cautiously, Molly got up and put her arms around the wet neck, her tears now tears of joy.

When they were both a little calmer, she led the filly over to the saddlebags and, with the aid of the carrots and apple and lavish praise, accustomed her to the feel of the rope on her body. By the time Molly saddled her riding horse, Lady had almost stopped shuddering at the touch of the rope. Molly could tie and untie it from her halter without an ear flipping.

"Trust me, Lady," she said as they stood at the gate. "Just keep trusting me and I promise you, you'll be happy. I won't ever hurt you. I love you, Lady."

The filly nuzzled her in answer, and the love and trust in her eyes made Molly surer than ever that she must find a way to bring Lady to the ranch house. On the long ride home she searched her mind desperately for a way to convince her father of Lady's worth.

The next few days passed pleasantly. Her visits to the filly were so successful she barely noticed the time she spent sewing with her mother, and the unchecked portion of fence faded from her mind. September seemd a lifetime away, and the nightmare of entering high school came second to her worry over her father and Lady.

Then one bright Wednesday morning, her mother had a suggestion that brought the nightmare close to her again. At breakfast, Mrs. Rogers said, "Today we're turning the ranch over to Dan to run. We're all going into town together."

"But the herd . . ." Molly began weakly.

"It can take care of itself for one day," her father said. "Today will be a holiday for all of us. It'll do us good."

Molly made no more objections, but her heart was heavy as she got into the car with her parents. She knew that whatever else was planned, the trip to town was bound to include a stop at the drugstore for her to see her "friends." She wondered if Paul and Ginger would even remember her.

Sure enough, after lunch, the shopping trips, and a visit to the grocery store, her father parked in front of the drugstore. "Time for a soda before we start home," he said.

Through the open door, she could hear the blaring of the jukebox and see the blur of couples in the back. "You go on back and talk to Paul and Ginger," her mother said, giving her a light shove. "There's plenty of time before we have to start back."

Molly walked slowly, searching the booths for a familiar face, but the only one she recognized was the cool blonde, Robin. Knowing that her parents were watching her, she headed for the poster, hoping that they wouldn't be able to see her there.

It offered her sanctuary for only a few moments, then the music stopped and quiet descended. Feeling suddenly exposed, Molly turned to the poster, staring at it but not seeing it. "Hi, Molly," a familiar voice said.

"Ginger," Molly gasped, so grateful that she felt foolish. "I didn't see you when I came in."

"Come on over to our booth," Ginger invited.

"Thanks," Molly said, feeling again the

little glow of hope that she might be able to make friends after all.

There were three other girls in the booth, but they moved over willingly and seemed friendly enough when Ginger made the introductions. Molly tried to keep track of their names, but her mind was a blank. She could only smile shyly and say, "Hi." Her feelings of inadequacy weren't helped when Robin joined them.

"Still trying to train your mustang for the gymkhana?" she asked.

"I'm not sure I'll be entering her," Molly stammered, feeling the red rising in her cheeks.

"I wouldn't bother," Robin said. "My father's buying me a top horse, and Ginger has a good one. Really, it would just be a waste of time to truck yours in."

Molly sat in humiliated silence, not knowing how to fight this unreasonable attack. The other girls had nothing to say either, and she wasn't sure whether they were silent out of a feeling of pity or disgust. Finally the jukebox started, and in a moment Robin left the booth.

"Wow," Ginger said, "you sure are popular with Robin, aren't you?"

"Yeah," the other girls chimed in.

Molly just stared at the scarred tabletop, too humiliated to answer, though she knew from their tone that they meant to be kind. While she was still trying to pull her courage together and make another try at conversation, Paul slid into the booth across from her.

"How's your filly coming along?" he asked.

Molly looked up. "Pretty well," she said. "I had a little trouble breaking her to lead because she was rope-shy, but she's all right now."

"What made her rope-shy?" Paul asked. "Was it just because she's a mustang?"

"No, it was more than that." Molly told him about finding the filly, and felt a little better when he really seemed interested. Her pleasure was short-lived, however, for in a few moments Paul looked up at the clock, muttered a few words about having to go home, and left. By this time Ginger and her friends were talking about the coming school year. Molly sat quiet and outside their conversation as it went from school to clothes to summer dances and the drill team, and from there to boys. It was almost a relief when she looked up and saw her smiling parents beckoning to her. She excused herself and almost ran away.

Living in town made the difference, she decided on the way home, a difference that she couldn't overcome. Ginger's friendliness was genuine, as was her invitation to Molly to call any time she came to town. But there was such a gulf between them. Molly thought of Lady and wondered if anyone could ever mean as much to her as the filly did; she was sure no one could.

Less than a week after Lady met the test of the rope, Molly decided she was ready for the next step in her education. The weather had turned hot and dry, surprisingly so for that early in the season. Every day the drying wind took more life from the plains. The green buffalo grass dried and cured like hay. It was still good for grazing, but Molly knew that new grass would have little chance to grow in the corral, and Lady would have to be moved even sooner than she'd expected.

She hobbled her riding horse and left him outside the corral to conserve all the grass she could. Then, with shaking hands, she pulled a length of rope through the ring on Lady's halter and knotted it in the middle to make reins. It was time to ride the filly, to teach her what being a tame horse meant.

To make it as easy as possible for Lady, Molly led her to the corral fence and climbed up beside her. The filly stood quiet, her gaze only mildly curious. Molly leaned one arm across her back, putting more and more weight on it. Lady looked at her, a little confused. Molly gave her a molasses cube.

For a few minutes more she hesitated, looking down at the unsuspecting filly and wondering how she would react. It would be so easy to undo all the trust she'd built up. Molly remembered all too well the violent plunging when the rope had been Lady's only enemy. But it must be done, and time was short.

Molly gathered the rope reins tight and slid her leg slowly across the filly's back, settling down on her as gently as she could. For a moment all she felt was the trembling that ran through Lady's body. "Easy, girl," she said, taking a handful of mane along with the reins. "It's all right. I won't hurt you."

The last words were whipped back as

Lady plunged forward, trying to escape the unfamiliar weight on her body. Molly tightened her legs against the filly's sides, knowing that it would add to her fear, but afraid she would fall off if she didn't. Lady ran furiously around the corral, narrowly missing the trees in her flight. When that didn't succeed, she began trying to buck.

At first, Molly's tight hold on the reins kept Lady's head up, so that her bucks were scarcely more than crowhops. Then Lady reared, high and wavering. For one horrible moment, Molly feared she would go over backward. She loosened the reins, clinging desperately to keep from sliding back over Lady's haunches.

The filly came down bucking. She was small and light, but what she lacked in bone-jarring weight she made up for in twisting speed. After three jumps, Molly knew she wouldn't be able to last. On the fourth plunge, she hurtled through the air and landed hard on the brittle grass.

Molly had been thrown and bucked off horses enough times to know that it was best to lie still for a few moments. She waited for the slight dizziness to leave and for her breath to return. Then, feeling a hundred small aches, she got up. Lady was standing a few yards away, breathing hard. She obviously hadn't connected the weight on her back with Molly, for she was easy to catch.

Molly took her time, petting Lady and talking to her, then she led her back to the corral fence. It took a while to get the filly to stand by the rails, but at last she relaxed, and Molly gathered the rope reins and slid aboard again. She stayed longer the second time and still longer the third, but the ground seemed harder each time she hit it.

The sun blazed down, and as Molly led the filly to the fence the fourth time, they were both dripping wet. Though she ached all over, Molly knew that Lady was in worse shape. The filly was limping a little and was so wet her chestnut coat looked almost black. Molly longed to give up and let her rest, but she knew that it wouldn't do any good. Lady had to fight until she was too tired to care. Then, when the panic was gone, there was a chance that she'd allow Molly on her back, and the fight would be over.

"At least," Molly told the horse before she mounted, "I hope you won't be afraid of me just because I'm on your back."

This time when she settled on the filly's back, Lady managed only two crowhops before she stopped. Molly sat still, not even daring to ease her hold on the reins. Lady took a step forward, then another, staggering a little in her exhaustion. Very gently, Molly leaned forward and rubbed the wet neck.

"You know me, Lady?" she said. "Can't you see that it's me on your back?"

The filly stopped and rolled one white-rimmed eye back at Molly, then tentatively she turned her head far enough to sniff Molly's knee. Molly slid off and led her over to the fence again. From there she climbed on and off the filly a dozen times. Finally she moved her away from the rails and vaulted on from the ground for the first time.

When she was sure that Lady understood, Molly walked her around and around the corral until she was completely dry and cooled. Then, and only then, did she let the thirsty filly wade in the cold spring to drink.

Hot and aching, Molly watched her enviously. The temptation was too great.

Molly took off her boots, and socks and jeans, and waded into the pool beside Lady. As soon as the cold water had eased some of her tiredness, she pulled a handful of the thick-leaved plants that grew in the spring and, using them like a washrag, bathed the filly.

Lady seemed to enjoy it. She waded into deeper water and stood still while Molly scrubbed away the marks of battle. Later she rolled on the brown grass, letting the sun warm her.

It was late afternoon when Molly left. Before going she vaulted onto Lady's back again and rode her slowly around the corral. She was pleased that the filly only looked back at her a few times and no longer seemed afraid.

"We're going to make it, Lady," she said. "I know we are. It won't be long now."

Chapter 10

Weary and sore from her battle with the filly, Molly went to bed as early as she could without arousing suspicion. Twice during the night the howling of the wind woke her, and then, toward dawn, a tremendous crash brought her scurrying from her bed to the window.

Lightning slashed the sky, flooding the wet landscape with white light, then plunging it again into rumbling darkness. Wind whipped the rain against the house as though it was trying to drive it through the boards and windows. Molly shivered, feeling sorry for all the animals on the plains, but thinking especially of Lady and the young calves.

As quickly as it had begun, the thunder and lightning ceased and the rain became hail. The pounding on the roof and walls was almost deafening. Outside the leaves were being torn from the trees. Molly went back to bed shivering, hoping that the filly had found some shelter under the canyon's rocky outcroppings.

Her mind told her that a horse that could survive three brutal Montana winters with a wild herd could survive a little rain and hail. But Lady was no longer a true wild horse, and, as the person who had tamed her, Molly felt responsible for her.

By the time she and her family got up, the storm had stopped entirely. Except for the wet earth and torn leaves, it might never have happened at all. Molly did her chores quickly, anxious to get to the canyon as soon as possible.

At breakfast, her father said, "I think we'd all better check the herd today. A storm like last night's doesn't disturb a range herd, but those cows aren't used to it. They just might have panicked and split up."

Molly nodded, wondering what excuse she could use for coming home by way of the canyon — alone. "That was quite a storm," she said.

"Hot as it's been, I'm not a bit surprised. We needed the rain." Her father headed for the door, with Molly right behind him.

Dan joined them at the barn, and they rode out together. It was cool and sunny, a perfect day for a ride, and Molly was enjoying it. She led them to the last place she'd seen the herd, pretty sure they wouldn't have strayed far.

But the plain was empty. Every way they looked there was nothing but waving prairie grass. "They were here yesterday," Molly said. "I'm sure it was right here."

"They may have headed for the creek to get under the trees," Dan suggested, reining Jackrabbit around.

As they neared the creek, they caught sight of the familiar red-and-white shapes, but instead of a calmly grazing herd the cows were scattered all over. Her father groaned. "Well," he said, "let's go."

They split up, moving through the brush and trees, gathering the cows into small bunches and herding them back to the plains. It was slow work, but finally Molly was sure there were no more cattle hiding in the brush of her section, and rode back to the main herd. While she waited for Dan and her father, she counted the herd — forty-two and six calves.

Quickly she counted again, reaching the same total. That left eight cows and one calf still unaccounted for. She shifted nervously in the saddle, looking for Dan and her father and hoping they would have the missing cattle. Dan rode up first, alone.

"No more?" Molly asked.

"I combed that brush. How many are still out?"

"Eight and one calf unless Daddy brings them in."

Her hope was shattered a moment later when her father appeared with only one cow. "That's the last one I could find," he said. "Did we get them all?"

Molly shook her head. "There are seven cows and a calf still missing. I counted twice."

"Well, we'd better look around for them. Molly, you follow the creek south, then cut back along the high ground. I'll go west. Dan, you go straight north and check the canyon sections. We can meet back here with the ones we find. I can't afford to lose one of those cows let alone seven, so look hard."

Molly rode south, relieved that her father had sent Dan to the canyon instead of taking that section himself. The filly was nearly ready to be introduced to him, but she didn't want them to meet by accident.

The ride south along the creek was disappointingly empty. She rode back along the ridges, watching closely for any sign of the cattle, but she was sure the cows hadn't come this way. Heavyhearted, she rode back toward the herd, still keeping to the high ground and stopping frequently to survey all directions. Her father was waiting when she rode up.

"You didn't see any either?" he asked.

Molly shook her head. "They didn't cross the creek. You have any luck?"

"Nope. They must have headed straight north. I sure hope Dan finds them. Something must have really set them off."

"What could have done it?" Molly asked.

"Who knows? The wind was blowing hard. It could have been a broken branch, a piece of tar paper from one of the shacks west of here, or just the thunder and lightning. A scared herd doesn't need much."

Molly looked at the quiet herd. "They look so peaceful now," she said.

"Maybe they'll never do it again. Let's ride along and see if we can meet Dan. He might need help."

They hadn't ridden far when they caught sight of Dan. Molly's heart lifted at the sight of the cattle. She counted seven and was straining her eyes, trying to locate the one missing calf. "He's got them all," she said, happily, "except the calf. I don't see it."

When she looked at her father, he wasn't smiling as she'd expected. "He's coming too slow," he said. "Something must be wrong."

They kicked their horses into a lope, heading for the distant group. As they neared it, Molly could see that all was not well. Two of the cows were limping badly and the missing calf was riding across Dan's horse, tied securely in place.

"What happened?" her father asked as they reined in beside Dan.

"Barbed wire. Up toward the northwest corner. The cows aren't too badly cut up, but this little fellow is going to need some care if he's going to grow up."

Molly felt sick when she looked at the calf.

His red-and-white hide was torn in a dozen places, and he lay so still he looked dead already. One of the cows came over and sniffed at him. He whimpered softly.

"How'd they get in the wire?" her father asked, dismounting to examine the cows for himself.

"The fence was down. Post was broken off and lying flat. I guess they didn't see it until they were into it. Tore themselves up to get loose. I propped the post up and re-strung enough to hold it till I can come out and replace that section."

"Lightning hit the post?" her father asked, remounting and cutting four cows out of the bunch.

"Don't think so. I can't say for sure, but from the looks of it, I'd say that post has been broken quite a while. Want me to take these four in?"

"You ride ahead with the calf and see if you can save him. I'll bring the four cows that are cut up. Molly you take the other three back down to the herd. Okay?"

Her father was looking her way, but Molly could only nod weakly. She reined her horse between the two bunches of cattle and slapped her leg to start the three cows on their way. They moved off briskly, as though eager to rejoin the herd. Though it made her feel worse, she looked back once, watching the slow progress of the limping cows. Dan and Jackrabbit had already disappeared toward the ranch.

Lightning hadn't broken the post. "Quite a while," Dan had said. Had the fence been down the day she was supposed to be checking it? She would never know. Dan could tell that the break wasn't a new one, but he'd never be able to tell her whether or not she was responsible for the hurt cattle.

The days she'd spent with the filly went through her mind. She could have checked it on any one of them. It would have meant less time with Lady, but what about the calf — if he died it would be her fault. The cows broke into a clumsy lope and went to join the herd.

Molly decided there was plenty of time to check the filly and catch up to her father before he reached the ranch with the injured cows. She turned her horse north and let him run for most of the way, knowing it wouldn't hurt him.

When she reached the corral, Lady greeted her warmly. But even the filly's nuzzling

couldn't wipe away the picture of the piti-
ful calf. She tied her horse and vaulted onto
the filly. Lady gave one light crowhop, then
trotted around the pasture as though she'd
been ridden for years.

"You're a good girl, Lady," Molly said,
feeling guilty about the rather brusque
treatment she was giving the horse. "I
don't blame you. It's my fault, all my fault.
I should have known something like this
would happen."

She petted the filly for a few moments,
then mounted her horse and headed for
home. She caught up with her father about
a half hour's ride from the ranch.

"Do you think the calf will be okay?"
Molly asked after they'd ridden a little while.

"Depends on how deep the cuts are, and
whether or not any tendons are cut in his
legs. At least we got to him before any in-
fection could get too far along."

They rode the rest of the way in silence.
Molly watched the limping cows and worried about the calf. In the back of her mind
were memories of the afternoon she'd spent
with Lady instead of riding on to check the
rest of the fence.

Chapter 11

When they reached the ranch, her father said, "You unsaddle the horses and put them in the corral for now — Jackrabbit too."

Molly took the reins of her father's horse and watched as he opened the barn door and urged the cows inside. As soon as the door closed behind him, she dismounted, untied Jackrabbit, and led the three horses into the corral.

Unsaddling seemed to take forever. Her fingers were stiff, and when she saw the small smears of blood on Dan's saddle, she felt sick. She set the two heavy saddles on the corral rail beside her own smaller one, hanging the bridles neatly over the horns. Then, dreading it, she went into the barn.

The cows had been put into separate stalls and were eating contentedly while Dan and her father doctored the torn places on their legs and flanks. Molly walked slowly from stall to stall, trying not to show her worry, but searching in every dim corner for the calf.

As soon as she was sure he wasn't in with any of the cows, she searched the two empty stalls. Her heart ached with each step. The calf wasn't there! She stood for a moment in the center aisle, watching the two men and thinking about the calf. It must be dead, and it was her fault. Guilt choked her. She ran from the barn, across the yard, and through the house to her room.

She threw herself on the bed and sobbed out her agony. There was no longer a question in her mind about the fence post. She was sure it had been down before the cows arrived, down the day that she should have been riding fence. It was her fault, her secret had cost the calf his life. At that moment there was a knock on her door.

"Molly, may I come in?" It was her father.

She sobbed out a yes, knowing that she would have to tell him now — the truth wouldn't help the calf, but it might ease some of her guilt.

"What's the matter?" he asked. "I saw you run out of the barn. What happened?"

"It's all my fault, Daddy," Molly sobbed. "I didn't check all the fence. I killed the calf. Oh, I'm so sorry!"

"Hold on now. What's all your fault?"

"I didn't get all the fence checked. I fell asleep and it was so late when I woke up. . . . If I'd ridden the rest of the way, it wouldn't have happened. . . . I'd have found the post and the calf would still be alive."

For a moment her father didn't speak, but she felt his hand on her shoulder, patting it gently. "Now, honey," he said, "first of all, the calf isn't dead. I don't — "

"But I looked for him," Molly interrupted. "He wasn't in the barn."

"You should have asked. Dan took him into the feed room so he could heat the water to wash him easier. He's still in there, all wrapped up. You can go see if you want."

Molly followed her father back out to the barn. Dan was in the feed room when they came in, bending over a blanket-shrouded form. "He's looking a little better," he said, without turning.

"Is he going to make it?" her father asked quietly.

"He's got a good chance. I'll watch him tonight, but I don't think there's much danger. They all came through surprisingly well."

"When do you think the post was broken?" her father asked, his eyes still on Molly.

"Who can tell? Before the rainstorm, I know, but how long before is anybody's guess. Why?"

"Just curious. Thanks, Dan." He turned away. "Come on, Molly," he said, "we've got some talking to do."

Her relief at seeing the calf gave way to fear. What she'd told her father had eased her conscience a little. But what about the filly? Would the truth destroy Lady? Molly tried to think of a way out, but nothing came except lies, and she was sorry now for the half-truths she'd already told.

Her father led her into the living room and patted the couch beside him. Through the window she could see her mother kneeling beside the front flower bed, working to repair the storm's damage. Suddenly she wished that she'd trusted her mother with her secret. She longed for someone to turn to, someone to give her aid and advice be-

fore she ruined everything. But it couldn't
be avoided, so she sighed and faced her
father.

"Now," he said, "about the fence. Why
didn't you get it all checked?"

"I told you — I fell asleep and you told
me to be home for supper, so I didn't have
time."

"Molly, that's not like you. Whether or
not the break occurred before that day
really isn't the important thing. Those cows
might have run through a perfect fence.
That we'll never know. The important thing
is that you neglected your job, and failed
to tell me about it."

"I'm sorry, Daddy."

"That's not enough. I have to know why,
Molly. You're not a little girl, you know
how important these cattle are. Why didn't
you tell me you'd only finished part of the
fence? You could have gone back the next
day."

"You wanted me to go to town with you."
Molly knew she was stalling, that she would
have to tell, but the words wouldn't come.
She thought only of the times her father
had threatened to shoot the wild horses or
round them up for the cannery. What if he

killed Lady? Fresh tears blurred her eyes.

"I'm waiting for the truth, Molly. You've been acting strangely ever since school got out this spring. What is it? Can't you tell me?"

"Oh, Daddy." Slowly, painfully, she sobbed out the whole story, telling him everything from the day Baron had led her to the nearly dead horse, to the few moments she'd spent riding her that morning. Then, exhausted and afraid, she waited for the explosion.

"You've been hiding a wild horse?" He sounded more stunned than angry.

"She's not a wild horse now, Daddy," Molly said, hope returning slightly. "She's even broken to ride."

"A wild horse. Molly, you know how I feel about mustangs. How could you?"

"I couldn't leave her to die out there, and she was too lame to go with the herd," Molly protested.

"She should have been destroyed then."

"But she's well now and gentle. Please, Daddy, give her a chance.

"All these weeks you've been lying to me and neglecting your work for a wild horse." He shook his head. "I just don't understand. We have good horses here. Why must you drag a wild one off the range and hide it? Why?"

"Because she's mine, Daddy, all mine. I've never had a horse of my own. She really belongs to me."

"I'd give you any of the horses we have, you know that. Or even buy you one, if that's all that bothers you. I just don't want a mustang around here."

"Jackrabbit was a wild horse."

"Jackrabbit belongs to Dan." Her father's face was set.

"But you haven't even seen her," Molly said, feeling the desperation of losing. "Why won't you even give her a chance? I love her, Daddy. I can't let her go. I need her!"

"What do you mean, you need her?" The question was almost an accusation.

Molly looked at him, knowing that he'd never understand the loneliness and fear of not belonging. He had her mother, they had each other, and anyway, she thought, they were too old to remember how it felt to be thirteen. The filly was as alone as she was, but there weren't any words that could explain it to her father. Somehow she would have to think of another reason, one he could understand.

She thought suddenly of the poster in the drugstore and her father's interest in it. "I need her to enter the gymkhana," she said. "All the kids I'll be going to school with are entering, and I've even told some of them about Lady. It would help me get acquainted."

Molly waited in breathless silence, knowing that this too was a lie, but vowing to make it the truth if her father would only spare Lady. He took a long time answering, his face unreadable. Finally, he sighed. "I'd like to see this mustang of yours," he said.

Fresh tears, this time from relief, filled her eyes. Molly hugged her father. "Oh, thank you, Daddy," she whispered. "Thank you."

"Hold on, now," he said. "I didn't say you could keep her. I don't see why you can't enter one of our horses in the gymkhana. But I'll look at her before I decide what should be done."

"Shall I bring her in?" Molly jumped to her feet.

"Not today. We've got our hands full

with the cows and the calf. Besides, it's late. Help your mother, and let me give this a little thought."

Molly went about her work happily, without complaining. She told her mother about the filly and was surprised at the pleasure her mother showed when she mentioned the gymkhana. Though it had only been a desperate excuse to Molly, both her parents seemed to think it was a wonderful idea. At supper that night her father promised to pick up a list of rules for her the next time he went in for supplies.

By the next morning her excitement had reached fever pitch. A visit to the barn assured her that the calf was much better, and her father asked her to take two of the cows back to the herd. Only the calf and his mother and one other cow remained to remind Molly of her mistake.

Baron whined at her when she came out of the barn, but Molly paused only a moment to pat him and say, "I'm sorry, fellow, but I don't think you'd better come along today. Your foot is getting better, but this might be a pretty rough trip. Maybe tomorrow you can go with Lady and me."

The old dog wagged his tail slowly, his

brown eyes sad and accusing. Molly knew that she'd neglected him since he'd led her to the filly, and she gave him an extra hug and promised that the next ride would include him.

She saddled her father's black horse and hung a lead rope on the saddle. A bag of oats, the curry comb and brush, and her pockets full of cubes completed her preparations. She turned the two cows loose and drove them out of the barn. Her father was standing by the corral.

"Now you be careful," he said, watching her mount. "Those wild ones can't be trusted and don't you forget it. I'll leave the corral gate open so you can ride right in and snub her."

"She's not that way, Daddy," Molly protested, knowing it was hopeless, but still wanting to defend Lady.

"I'm not going to take any chances, Molly. I know a lot more about horses than you do."

Molly mounted without replying and started the cows on their way. It was a long, slow ride. The cows were still sore and Molly didn't push them, though she longed to race all the way to the canyon.

Today was the day she'd been waiting for, and she wanted to share her fears and happiness with the filly. Still, determined to make no more mistakes, she forced herself to take the time to count the cows and make sure that none had strayed since yesterday. When she was convinced that all was well, she hurried the black horse north, happy that this would be her last ride to the canyon to visit Lady.

The filly welcomed her warmly, as though she sensed Molly's excitement. While Lady ate the oats, Molly used the curry comb and brush to make her look her best. Before they set off for the ranch, Molly mounted Lady and rode her around and around the corral.

It didn't take long for Lady to learn to stop when Molly pulled on the rope. Now that her fears were gone, she seemed to like being ridden. "I wish I could ride you home," Molly said, rubbing her neck, "but I guess I'd better not."

The filly seemed surprised when Molly opened the corral gate and tied it back against the fence, but she didn't try to pull away, even when Molly mounted the black horse. Molly led Lady slowly at first, letting her stop and look whenever she wanted to, matching the black's gait to that of the filly. Soon, however, the filly settled down and kept her head close to Molly's knee whether they walked or loped.

But as soon as they came in sight of the ranch, Lady's behavior began to change. She slowed, hanging back against the rope a little, forcing the black horse to drag her. Molly tried to soothe her, but she only half listened; mostly she watched the buildings below fearfully.

Molly's pleasure vanished and a tight knot of fear replaced it. The filly was afraid, afraid of the ranch and of the people on it. Molly's plans for a proud entrance to show her horse off to her parents faded. Instead she had to figure out a way to get Lady down to the corral quietly so she'd have a chance to get her used to things before her parents came out to see her.

Chapter 12

No amount of coaxing or urging seemed
to work. Finally, in desperation, Molly dismounted, dropping the reins. She knew that
her father's well-trained cow pony would
never stray more than a few feet as long as
his reins trailed on the ground. That left
her free to turn her whole attention to the
frightened filly.

As soon as Molly was on the ground
petting and talking to her, Lady seemed
to relax. Molly took her time. She led Lady
along the ridge above the ranch, letting her
look as long as she wanted. Then, slowly,
she began leading her down toward the back
of the barn. Lady came willingly enough,

her head over Molly's shoulder as though for reassurance.

Molly scanned the house and barn carefully and was relieved to see that no one had come out yet. They were close to the corral now. Molly reached up to caress the velvety muzzle, her confidence returning.

As they approached the open gate of the corral, Molly heard the familiar squeak of the laundry room door and started to turn. With a happy bark, Baron came racing out to greet her. "Down, Baron!" she shouted, feeling the electric shock of fear that went through the filly when she saw the dog.

Baron dropped obediently, but the damage had been done. Before the filly crashed by her, Molly caught a glimpse of the horrified look on her mother's face. Lady's shoulder caught her and Molly hit the grass hard. The sun blackened, then came back hotter and stronger than before. Slowly, painfully, she struggled to her knees.

Looking first toward the house, she saw her mother still standing in the door, then, a little dizzily, she dragged herself up and began searching for the filly. It took only a moment to locate her. Lady was in the corral, backed as far away from the dog as she could get, ears flat against her head and teeth bared, ready to do battle. Molly started toward her, limping a little.

"Stand back, Molly. I'll take care of this." It was her father's voice.

Molly glanced over her shoulder and immediately forgot her aches and pains. Her father was on the back steps, his hunting rifle in his hand. . . . "No!" she screamed. "No, Daddy!" Then she ran for the corral.

She heard her father shouting to her to get away and give him a clear shot, but she closed her ears to everything outside the corral — the filly was the only thing in her world at that moment. Lady didn't move as Molly ran through the open gate. Her white-ringed eyes were fastened on the dog, and her big teeth seemed to gleam in the sun. Fearing that her father wouldn't give her a chance to explain, Molly didn't slow her run until she could almost touch the filly.

"Easy, Lady. Please, girl, it's all right." Molly pleaded, but to her horror, the filly began to rear.

There was no time to hesitate, for Molly knew that if Lady reared to her full height, her father would have a clear shot at her.

Molly jumped and caught the filly's halter, pulling her back down. For a moment, Molly's heart stopped. Lady was trying to pull away, fighting for her head. Then, as though she suddenly recognized her, Lady stopped. She stood, trembling and breathing hard, her head pressed firmly against Molly's chest.

Molly clung to her, barely able to stand now. Relief and fear raced through her in waves, and tears ran unnoticed down her cheeks to drip onto the filly's tangled mane. Time seemed to stand still until the bang of the gate behind her brought them both back to reality. Still keeping a firm hold on the filly's halter, Molly turned to face her father.

"What are you trying to prove?" he demanded. "Get away from that crazy animal right now."

"No," Molly said, shaking all over, but standing her ground. "She's not wild or crazy, Daddy. She was just scared. Baron scared her."

"She could have killed you." He still held the rifle, but he had lowered it a little.

"When she was hurt and I was trying to get her on her feet, I told Baron to attack her, just to scare her, and I guess she hasn't forgotten it. She had good reason to be afraid of him."

"Where's the horse you rode out?"

"Up on the ridge. Lady was afraid, so I thought she'd feel safer if I led her down alone. After all, Daddy, she's never seen anything like this before. She's tame when we're alone. Watch, I'll ride her and show you."

"No, you don't! I don't want you taking any more chances. Go up and bring the black horse down."

"You won't hurt Lady?" Molly asked, still not moving away from the filly. "Promise me, Daddy. You said you'd give her a chance, and this wasn't her fault."

"All right, Molly. I'm not going to do anything now. We'll talk about it after lunch." He left the corral and whistled for Baron.

Molly stayed in the corral until her parents and the dog were safely inside, then she unsnapped Lady's lead rope with shaking hands. The filly's eyes followed her pleadingly, as though she knew that she'd done something wrong and was sorry. Molly rubbed her soft neck and twitching ears. "It's all right, girl," she said. "I know you're sorry. It wasn't your fault. Things will be okay now, you'll see. They have to be!"

Reluctantly, Molly slipped between the corral rails and walked up the hill, where the black horse was still peacefully cropping grass. As she walked, she tried to think. What had happened in front of her father was the worst possible beginning for Lady, but Molly couldn't think of any way to change the bad impression her wild horse had made.

She led the black horse down the hill and inside the barn. She unsaddled him, then took a bucket of oats out to Lady. The filly seemed calmer now, and after a few minutes, Molly left her to go inside. Dan was sitting at the table with her parents. She washed the dirt off her hands and face, and joined them for lunch with a heavy heart.

"She's filled out well," Dan said. "Doesn't even look like the same little animal."

Molly was unprepared for this disclosure. She glanced at her father, but when he showed no anger, she knew they had been talking about her while she was up getting the black horse. "She's changed inside too," Molly said, eager to talk to someone who might understand. "Lady really cares about me. You saw her today. She was scared, but she didn't try to fight me in the corral, not when she knew it was me."

"Yes, I saw it all from the barn. She's your horse all right, maverick, no one else could have handled her."

"I think she's a dangerous horse. She could have killed you." Her father's voice was cold.

"She didn't mean to. It was Baron. I'll work with her so she won't be afraid of him. You'll see — she trusts me." Fear and unhappiness closed Molly's throat.

"I'm not trying to be unkind to you, Molly." Her father's tone was gentler. "I just don't want you hurt. That's a wild animal. You're all we've got, honey. We want to take care of you."

"Daddy, I could get hurt riding any horse, any time. I'd have to live in a cage to be safe all the time. Lady loves me. She'd never hurt me on purpose."

Silence settled over the table, a heavy, frightening silence that seemed to bode no good for Lady. Molly pushed her food around on her plate. Her back ached from her fall, but she dared not rub it or even stretch for fear her parents would blame the filly even more.

Finally her father cleared his throat and looked at her mother. "Well, Annie," he said, "What do you think?"

Molly turned to her mother, pleading wordlessly. But instead of giving an opinion, her mother turned to Dan. "How about it, Dan? Do you think Molly will be safe with her Lady?"

Dan stirred his coffee for a moment. "I'd trust my life to Jackrabbit," he said. "I have many times. He was wild once, but he isn't now. A wild horse can make the choice, and if they give themselves to a person they're better than any corral-raised horse. I think the filly has given herself to Molly."

Molly thanked him with her eyes, knowing how hard it had been for him to talk so freely about himself and his love for Jackrabbit. Only his love for her and his understanding of what she felt for Lady could have broken through his high wall of reserve. She looked at her mother, hoping that she had listened and would heed Dan's words.

140

"Well," her mother began, doubt still plain in her voice, "if you promise not to take any risks . . . Maybe we would let you try for a little while, see if she does work out."

"Till the gymkhana?" Molly asked, thinking that that would give her almost six weeks.

"I'll make you a promise," her father said. "If the filly can prove herself by getting a ribbon at the gymkhana, I'll try to forget she's been a mustang. But no foolish chances, Molly. If she can't be trained safely and properly, she goes back to the wild herd right away."

Molly nodded, too relieved to speak, hope and fear filling her. The filly was hers! Six weeks were a long time, and with the filly so close, she could work with her every day — it would be long enough! She began to eat her lunch, not even noticing that the food had grown cold.

After lunch, Molly took a long time leading Lady all around the ranch buildings, through the barn, and even down the path to Dan's cabin. Now that she was over her first fright, Lady seemed more curious than afraid. She followed Molly willingly, her eyes and delicate nostrils exploring each new sight and smell.

The tour completed to her satisfaction, Molly took Lady back to the corral and asked Dan to begin the second lesson about ranch life. This one took a great deal longer, but before sunset Lady had endured the touch of Dan, and Molly's father and mother. She was still afraid, but with Molly's hand on her neck she stood her ground. It pleased Molly to see the surprise in her father's face. Lady had a long way to go, but she had taken the first steps.

"Tomorrow," she told the filly when she came out to say good night, "you're going to have to start getting used to Baron. You may not realize it, but he helped me save your life. I think you should give him another chance. Besides, there will be dogs at the gymkhana, and you'll have to learn to ignore them."

Though it had been a very rough day, sleep was a long time coming, and when Molly did drift off, her dreams were troubled. She and Lady seemed to run forever, full of fear, and always just ahead of some horrible menace that they couldn't quite see.

Sometime before dawn, Molly woke, bathed in perspiration, her heart pounding wildly. The dream faded, but from the darkness outside she heard a plaintive whinny that she recognized immediately. Quickly, she pulled on her shoes and robe and tiptoed through the sleeping house, grateful that her parents hadn't been wakened by the filly.

Overhead the stars were cold and distant. Lady stood at the far side of the corral, her head high, looking off toward the plains. Molly knew that the filly was looking for her friends, the wild horses. She had to call twice before Lady would come to be comforted, but when she did come, Lady seemed grateful for the company.

Molly too looked out over the rolling prairie, watching the shadowy ripple of the grass under the prairie wind. She couldn't help wondering if Lady did belong out there instead of in the corral. She was safer here, for there were always deep snows and freezing winters, summer droughts and angry ranchers to plague the wild herds. But was she happier? Or was the corral a prison, and had Molly become her jailer?

From the front of the house, where he was now tied, Baron barked at some small night intruder and the filly trembled. Molly soothed her, talking softly of the many things they could share now that she had come to the ranch. Lady quieted, but in her heart Molly began to worry anew.

The six weeks, which had seemed so long at lunch, now appeared impossibly short. Lady had so many fears and so far to go before she could ever compete with other horses. Just to prepare her to enter a gymkhana arena was more than Molly had dared to consider. To add the condition that she must take a ribbon in one of the events was asking the impossible.

Molly stayed with her horse till dawn began fading the stars. Hopeless or not, she knew she'd have to try. She loved her Prairie Lady, and she couldn't give her up without a fight. When she got back to her room, she looked out the window and saw that the filly was now standing and looking toward the house, as though she missed her too. It made her worry a little easier to bear.

Chapter 13

In the morning, Molly decided that Lady's reconciliation with Baron might as well come first. The old sheep dog resented being tied, and it showed in the full dish of dog food he refused to touch. She was sorry now that she hadn't taken Baron with her to the box canyon, where Lady could have reacted to him as violently as she wished without having her life threatened with a rifle. Now, however, it was too late for such "might-have-beens."

Sighing, Molly went out and untied Baron, telling him to heel as they came around the house. Lady was eating the oats Molly had brought her, but as soon as she caught the dog's scent, she whirled to face him.

Molly paused just outside the corral and began petting Baron, and talking to both animals. The filly was in the center of the corral, ears back and teeth bared, ready to do battle with the dog she remembered had tried to attack her. Molly ignored the fighting stance and went on talking quietly, this time directly to Lady.

First one ear came forward, then the other. Then her teeth no longer showed and the hard tension slowly ebbed from her neck and shoulders. Baron watched her curiously. As a country dog, he'd been around horses all his life. He liked some of them and tolerated the rest, but he'd never before met one that hated and feared him the way Lady did.

Finally, when the situation seemed pretty well relaxed, Molly slipped into the corral, bringing Baron with her. Again the filly prepared for attack, and again Molly stopped and talked to both animals until the tension eased. As she talked, she was conscious of the worried eyes watching her from the house and barn, and they didn't help her own nervousness at all.

This time when the filly had relaxed,

Molly told Baron to stay and went over to Lady. She talked to Lady, petted her, and fed her molasses cubes and a few small pieces of carrot that she'd taken from the kitchen.

Slowly, a cautious step at a time, Molly and Lady crossed the few yards of hard-baked prairie soil to the spot where the dog waited patiently. Timidly, the filly extended her slender nose to touch the dog's soft, graying muzzle. Molly stepped back, leaving the two of them to get acquainted in their own time, hoping that their love for her would be bond enough to bring them together in a peaceful friendship.

As though sensing her feelings, the two circled each other warily, the dog not pressing too closely and the filly standing her ground. It took most of the morning, but by noon Baron was sleeping peacefully in the corral while the filly finished her oats and then drowsed trustingly in the sun. Molly went confidently in to lunch.

Her parents were less impressed with her morning's accomplishments than she was. Still, her father was less hostile when he mentioned the filly and even called her Lady instead of "that horse" or "the mustang." After lunch, he told her mother to stay at the table and called Molly into the living room.

"I suppose," he began, "you've been too busy with Lady to remember, but I think we have a couple of birthday presents to deliver."

Molly gasped. "Oh, Daddy," she said. "I'm so glad you remembered. I'll go get them."

The presentation was brief and the singing loudly off key, but her mother's smile made it all seem very important. The robe and slippers were admired and modeled, and Molly did the dishes alone while her parents drank coffee together in the living room. It gave her a good feeling to hear them laughing and talking together so happily.

In the afternoon, Dan helped her find a bridle small enough for Lady's delicate head. After considerable consultation, they decided to use the light snaffle bit that Dan had kept as a souvenir of his days of quarter-horse racing.

The finished bridle looked a little strange by western standards, but it was as small and light as they could manage, and that would make it easier for Lady to accept. Molly carried it to the corral proudly. As Dan watched her from the fence, she let the filly sniff it over.

"Have you still got that half an apple?" Dan asked, when she'd removed Lady's halter.

Molly nodded.

"Rub it across the bit a couple of times, then let her eat it. That'll make the bit a little easier for her to take."

Molly was grateful for Dan's help, for she realized how much Lady had to learn. The bridle was only the first step in teaching her the lessons of obedience, which she needed to enter the gymkhana and get accepted by Molly's father.

The filly took the bit willingly enough, tasting it and chewing it slightly while Molly made final adjustments on the bridle. Lady shook her head several times, then seemed to accept it. Molly led her around the corral a few times, then, without saying anything, crossed the reins on Lady's withers and vaulted onto her back.

She sensed rather than heard her father's gasp of surprise, but she ignored him. She rode Lady around and around the corral,

stopping every few yards to accustom the
filly to the feel of the bit. At first Lady
fought a little, resisting the pressure on her
sensitive mouth, but she soon learned that
the pain ceased when she stopped fighting.
From then on, the slightest tightening of
the reins brought her to an abrupt halt.

"Let her out, Dan," Molly called.

Dan hesitated for only a moment, then
swung the gate open before Molly's father
could object. Molly leaned forward, urging
the filly to walk through the gate. Lady
trotted out delicately. Molly let her go
where she pleased, not trying to teach her
to neck-rein as yet. As she rode past her
father, she waved to reassure him. He lifted
his hand halfheartedly but didn't order her
back to the corral, for which she was grateful.

In a burst of bravery, she turned Lady
away from the ranch buildings and whistled
for Baron to join them. Lady shied a little
when the big sheep dog loped up, but Molly
held her easily. The three of them went up
the hill together.

When they reached the top, Molly felt
the filly begin to tremble. Lady stopped of
her own accord and stood sniffing the wind

almost hungrily. Molly thought of turning back but hesitated, wanting to trust the filly now. Baron ran ahead, searching for a rabbit to chase or a gopher to bark at. The wind lifted Lady's mane, flipping it across Molly's hand, tickling her. She caught it lightly in her free hand.

Suddenly, Lady leaped forward, almost unseating Molly. Only the handful of mane saved her. Lady was running in a way Molly had never dreamed she could. Head down, she seemed to fly. Her slender legs skimmed the earth so smoothly it was like riding the wind. Molly leaned forward, going with her instead of trying to stop her.

The wind-driven mane no longer tickled, it snapped like sleet in her face, but she barely felt the stinging. The speed was intoxicating. She was a part of her horse for the first time, bound to her by the chain of love and complete accord. The rushing air whipped tears from her eyes, and dried them before they could run down her cheeks.

Then, when her hands were numb from holding the reins and mane, the violent speed began to ebb. For the first time since Lady's plunge forward, Molly thought of the turf beneath the filly's driving hooves. She remembered the danger of gopher holes and hidden ridges that could break the legs of galloping horses.

Shaking her head to clear the fog of exhilaration, Molly sat up and forced her aching fingers to tighten the reins. Lady slowed to a walk immediately, her sides heaving violently from the long run. Molly pulled Lady around, careful to press the outside rein against the filly's sweat-foamed neck.

As Lady plodded quietly along, Molly's knees began to shake. Her arms and hands felt so weak she could scarcely hold the reins. Even Jackrabbit, who was the fastest horse on the ranch, had never run like that with her. Baron had been left far behind. When she'd stopped Lady, Molly had been able to see the creek a short way ahead of them. How fast had they gone? Molly had no way of knowing. She brushed away the foam on Lady's neck and shoulders and remembered the burning wind on her face.

They met Baron, his tongue lolling out, heading home. He'd started to follow the filly's wild flight, then given up. Lady stopped to touch noses with her new-found friend, then walked on, the dog beside her.

They stayed that way until Lady stepped obediently through the corral gate.

Molly slid off, her legs still shaking a little from the strain and excitement. She closed the gate and slipped off the bridle, petting and praising the weary filly. Then she went to the barn for a cloth to wash away the hardened ridges of sweat on Lady's shoulders and back.

Her father followed her back to the corral. "What happened?" he asked. "Did you have trouble?"

"No, Daddy. I just let her run until she was tired." Molly dipped a pail into the water trough. "She was easy to stop."

"You shouldn't have taken her out like that. You don't know what she'll do."

"Daddy, she's the fastest horse I've ever ridden. It's like flying when she runs."

"You just be careful. I know you think she's tame, and I admit she acts tame now, but the wildness is still there. It can come out any time, and it will — when you least expect it."

Molly didn't argue. She went on washing the filly until her red coat was like satin. Then she combed the tangles from her mane and tail. When Molly was all finished, she stepped back to admire the horse. "You look almost like a racehorse, Lady," she said, "except you're so little."

The filly nickered softly and began pawing the dust daintily. Molly watched as Lady lowered herself to the ground, and with obvious pleasure, rolled back and forth in the warm dust.

"Lady!" Molly shouted furiously. "Oh, how can you?" When the filly got up and shook part of the dust off, Molly began to laugh. Her polished racehorse had become a typical range horse and she looked better that way.

Chapter 14

The month of July seemed to be passing with unbelievable speed. Each day Molly worked with Lady, teaching her to carry a saddle and to neck-rein like a cow pony. She rode her out to check the new herd of cattle and on the long tours of the fences. She even persuaded her father to let her use Lady when they had to round up the old herd and drive them to the road to meet the Jenner-Simmons trucks.

Except for her small size, Lady was beginning to look and act like an average cow pony. She had the inborn "cow sense" that was prized in all stock horses, and she made up for her smallness by being quicker on her feet than any horse except Jackrabbit. Nothing on the ranch seemed to frighten her. Molly had almost forgotten the filly's natural timidity when she set off with Dan and her father to round up the cattle in the south pasture.

It was barely dawn when they left the barn, all wrapped in sweatshirts, though it was the middle of summer. By the time they located the main body of the herd, the sun was starting its climb and the sweatshirts were tied behind their saddles. The cattle were fat and healthy, but Molly could appreciate her father's constant desire to improve his stock.

These cattle were mostly of Hereford ancestry, but traces of other breeds showed in their longer legs and thinner bodies. They looked larger, but would weigh less than the short, blocky purebreds that grazed in the northern pastures. In fact, Molly thought, they were almost as scrawny as most of the wild horses she'd seen.

It was well past noon before her father decided that all the strays had been found. They had gathered the herd near the creek, and as soon as the last stray had been rounded up, all three rode toward the inviting shade. They unsaddled their tired horses and let them drink and graze while they ate the food Mrs. Rogers had brought down from the ranch in the jeep.

After they ate, they rested for almost an hour, dreading the hot, dusty drive to the gate, just south of the ranch house, where they were to meet the trucks. Finally, Molly's father looked at his watch and got up. They saddled the horses and mounted in a companionable silence. "The trucks are due in about an hour," her father said, "so we'll have to push them right along."

Molly nodded, pleased to see that Lady and Jackrabbit seemed much fresher than her father's mount. Shouting and swinging a rope, Molly helped start the herd moving, then she and Lady were kept busy watching for strays and pushing the stragglers.

With every step the cattle threw up billows of dust from the dry grass. Molly's eyes stung and her throat burned. Often, when the filly turned aside and ran out from the herd, Molly couldn't even see what she was pursuing. But Lady's instincts were excellent.

Between the dust and the constant bawling of the cattle, Molly soon lost track of time and distance. Mostly she left the reins loose on Lady's neck, trusting her to do her job. It came as a shock when she realized that the herd had stopped and the dust was settling.

Dan rode up, his teeth gleaming white in his dust-crusted face. "Say, she's a natural, isn't she?" he said. "She's already better than half the cow ponies in the state."

"She's one smart horse." Molly agreed. "Wonder where the trucks are," she said, looking around.

"They'll be along. Be glad of a minute's rest." Dan held out a canteen. "Thirsty?"

Molly crossed the reins loosely on Lady's withers and took the canteen. "Thanks. I feel like I've chewed my way through an acre of dirt." She drank, then poured a little water on her handkerchief and tried to wipe the dust from her face.

"You're making mud," Dan observed.

Molly was so busy with the canteen that she didn't hear the rattle and bang of the cattle trucks as they came up the hill. She was just handing the canteen back to Dan when the first truck roared into view over the hill. A shudder shook Lady. Molly dropped the canteen and grabbed wildly for the reins. But it was too late.

Lady jumped away from the snorting trucks so quickly that Molly almost flipped off over her haunches. Then, Lady began to run. Molly clung desperately for a moment, fighting to regain her balance and get into rhythm with her horse. That accomplished, she began trying to catch at the trailing reins.

Lady was running into the wind, which helped keep the reins from dragging under her hooves and tripping her. But Molly knew that their luck couldn't hold forever. Sooner or later one of her driving hooves would land on a rein and Lady would somersault over the hard ground.

Holding on with one hand, Molly leaned forward, trying to reach the snapping leather. Twice it brushed her fingers, but each time it was whipped away before she could catch hold. Then, as her hold on the saddle was beginning to slip, she caught one rein. She began to pull hard, trying to stop Lady or force her into a tight circle to slow her.

For a moment nothing changed, then almost as suddenly as she'd started, Lady slid to a halt. Shakily, Molly leaned forward to catch the other rein. She relaxed for a second, letting relief drive out the paralyzing fear. For the first time, she became aware of the hoofbeats behind her. She reined the filly around just as Dan pulled Jackrabbit to a sliding stop beside her. Farther away, Molly saw her father spurring his horse after her too.

"You okay?" Dan asked.

Molly nodded, still too weak to speak. Her father thundered up.

"What happened?" he asked as soon as he was sure Molly was unhurt.

"It was my fault," Molly said quickly, knowing that he would blame Lady. "I was washing the dust off my face and I didn't hear the trucks."

"She ran away?" The edge of fury was in his tone.

"Not exactly. I mean, if I'd had a hold on the reins, I could have stopped her, but I wasn't holding them and — "

"You mean she was running free?"

"I finally caught one rein and she stopped real easy."

"Of all the brainless . . . You could have been killed! Why didn't you jump clear?"

"I was afraid she'd step on a rein and kill herself."

"I should have shot that horse the first time I saw her. She's crazy."

"She was just scared. She's never seen a truck before, Daddy."

"Molly, you can't go through life hoping you won't get killed every time she sees something new and panics. It just won't work. You'll have to get rid of her."

"But, Daddy, you promised." Sick fear spread through her like a disease.

"I warned you — if it was going to be too dangerous — Dan, where were you?" He turned on Dan with the same fury, but Dan didn't seem to notice it.

"I was right there, but I couldn't catch that little deer no matter how hard I spurred old Jackrabbit. That's the fastest horse I've seen in a long time."

Dan's calm manner seemed to soothe Molly's father. After a moment, he said, "Take her back to the house, Molly. We can load without you."

"Please, Daddy, I'd rather take her back to the herd. I want her to get used to trucks."

"And have her panic again?" The anger came back.

"I'm sure I can handle her now. It wouldn't have happened at all if I'd been paying attention to what I was doing."

"Of all the . . . oh, suit yourself." He

yanked the panting black horse around and headed back toward the herd.

Molly started after him, but Dan waved her back. "Let him go, maverick," he said. "It's not you he's mad at, or even the filly. He was afraid you'd get killed, and he loves you. His fear turned to anger — but it'll cool before long."

Dan and Molly started back slowly, the two horses still breathing hard, their dusty coats now streaked with sweat. As they rode, Molly thought of what Dan had said about Lady. "Is Lady really so fast?" she asked at last.

"Jackrabbit's no racehorse, but he's plenty fast, and she was leaving him with every bound."

Molly smiled as she pictured herself racing Lady one day, and winning, so her father would be proud to let her keep the filly. Then she pushed the daydream away and settled down to getting Lady to approach the trucks. It was a long, hot afternoon, and by the time the last cow and calf had been hazed up the ramp, Lady had lost her fear.

They were all tired, and rode home and unsaddled in weary silence. Her mother called to Dan from the house, asking him to join them for supper. As Molly carried a pail of oats to her filly, her father came over. "I'll keep my promise," he said, "but if she doesn't prove herself at the gymkhana, I'll sell her to the highest bidder. She can be a racehorse or go to the cannery, but I won't bring her home without a ribbon. She's just not trustworthy, Molly, and all the love and understanding in the world won't change the wild habits she has."

"I'll change her, Daddy," Molly said, though her heart was heavy. If one truck could frighten Lady, what would happen when she was surrounded by people and cars at the gymkhana? It seemed even more hopeless than before.

"Don't tell your mother what happened, it'll just worry her. Remember what I said, though, and be more careful! One more stunt like today, and you might not get to the gymkhana to prove it."

"Yes, Daddy." Molly blinked back her tired tears.

Supper was a quiet meal, but her mother didn't seen to notice or, if she did, attributed it to their weariness. Only Dan sensed Molly's misery and tried to comfort her with his understanding glances. But this time just understanding wasn't enough; she needed the assurance that the filly would always be hers.

The days passed. Molly made two trips to town with her parents, braving the crowd at the drugstore. Her father had picked up a booklet of the events and the rules, and Molly filled out the entry blanks for the events she'd decided to enter.

After much thought and several consultations with Dan, she decided that her best chance of winning a ribbon would come from using the filly's blazing speed. This was especially true since the events were split into three divisions: riders under twelve; juniors, twelve through sixteen; and adults, seventeen and older. Since Molly wasn't quite fourteen, that meant she'd be competing against many older and more experienced gymkhana riders.

The first event she chose was the barrel-and-stake race. This involved taking stakes, one at a time, from one barrel to another, all at top speed. The first rider to get all six stakes in the second barrel and ride back across the finish line would be the winner.

Her second choice was the pole-bending

contest. Though she'd never seen one, the pamphlet explained that six poles would be set up in a line, with approximately a horse's length between them. Each rider would race down the line, bending in and out between the poles, turn around the last pole, and weave back. It was a timed event, but the horse's grace was even more important than his speed, since a knocked down or skipped pole meant the rider would be disqualified.

Picking a third event to enter was the hardest of all, but Molly wanted to enter as many events as possible to give Lady every chance to win a ribbon. There were plenty of races and games, but a good half of them required a partner, and some involved dismounting and leaving the horse alone while the rider picked things up. Molly was sure that Lady would be too frightened to stand alone. Dan finally suggested that she enter the barrel race and Molly agreed, though she'd heard Robin mention it several times when she forced herself to talk to the unfriendly girl.

For the last two weeks before the gymkhana, Molly and Lady practiced on the flat area behind Dan's cabin. Two empty barrels were set at the proper distance, and Molly carried stakes back and forth until Lady learned not to mind the occasional banging of wood against her sides or legs.

The pole-bending event was a little harder to duplicate, but by using all of her mother's brooms and mops, and setting them up in sand-filled pails, Molly managed a five-pole stretch to practice on.

Lady seeemed to enjoy the pole-bending and was soon racing through the line at a speed Molly would never have urged her to try. Molly was sure her filly would have the advantage over the bigger, clumsier horses, and she pinned her hopes on winning a ribbon in the pole-bending event. Of all the events, that was the one that should produce the ribbon that would make her father admit that Lady was a worthy horse.

Lady found the cloverleaf barrel race easy too. She soon had the pattern learned and required little guidance. Lady cut so close to the barrels that Molly had trouble keeping her inside foot from knocking them over. Lady needed no urging; she seemed to sense that it was a race, though no other horse competed against her.

Since they had no stopwatch, Molly had

no idea how Lady's time compared with the results of last year's gymkhana, but she was sure that her filly was fast. Still, just being fast here wasn't enough. It was easy for Lady to do her best here on the quiet, familiar plains with only Dan and Baron to watch her. The test would come when she was in the middle of a crowd of screaming, cheering people.

The week before the gymkhana, Dan began pounding on the empty oil barrels, whistling, and shouting, trying to condition Lady to noise and confusion. But even when Lady learned to ignore him, Molly wasn't too hopeful. She couldn't help remembering the filly's reaction to the cattle trucks and, deep down, she realized that she too was afraid of the crowd.

Chapter 15

The day of the gymkhana dawned clear but windy. Molly, too nervous and worried to sleep, sat by her window and watched the streaks of morning spread across the sky. The corral was empty; Lady, groomed to shining perfection, had her own stall now and was quite content in the barn with the other saddle horses.

Molly stared out over the rippling brown prairie, thinking of her horse. What if she lost today? Her father had said that he'd sell Lady. Molly felt sick inside at the thought. No one else would understand or care about Lady — they might beat or neglect her. Molly tried not to think about the other part of the threat, but it was hard to ignore the thought of the cannery.

She paced her room, biting at her fingers and worrying about Lady's future. The longer she thought about it, the more sure she was that she couldn't risk Lady's life. She dressed slowly, dreading what she decided she must do. The sun was over the horizon when she tiptoed through the sleeping house and out into the windy dawn.

The barn was quiet, but Lady whickered as soon as she caught Molly's scent. Her friendly trust made Molly feel disloyal. She carried oats to all the horses while Lady ate hers, then she snapped a lead rope on Lady's halter and led her to the door. Right or wrong, Molly was sure that Lady would be safer with the wild horses than gambling on winning a ribbon at the gymkhana.

Since she hadn't too much time, Molly merely led the filly to the ridge above the house and slipped off her halter. "You're free, Lady," she said, blinking back her tears. "Run toward the mountains and I'll ride out later and open the gate for you."

The filly stood, watching her with curious eyes, not afraid, only confused. Molly gave her a little push. "Go on," she said. Lady danced a few steps away, then looked back. "Scram," Molly cried, waving her arms and choking on the sobs that shook her body.

Lady hesitated a moment, then began to lope away, looking back every few strides. Molly watched her for only a minute, then turned and ran back down the hill as fast as she could. If she stayed she knew she'd be unable to resist the impulse to call Lady back. She was almost at the barn when she felt the filly's soft muzzle hit her back. "Oh, Lady," Molly said, turning and burying her face in the tangled mane. Lady nuzzled her, then walked quietly back into the barn.

"Hello, maverick." Molly jumped as Dan stepped out of Jackrabbit's stall. "I thought you might be here," he said.

"I was trying to turn Lady loose," Molly said, "but she won't go."

"She loves you. Why do you want her to go?"

"What else can I do?" Molly asked miserably. "If she loses today, Daddy said he'd sell her. She might even end up going to the cannery. At least if she's with the wild herd, she'll be safe."

"And when they round up the wild horses what happens to her then? She's not branded, and now that you've gentled her she might not fight so hard to be free."

"But she'll get wild again — she'll have to."

"You'll gamble on that, but not on her trust and your love and training? I think she made her choice up there on the hill." Dan's eyes were kind.

"You saw us?"

"She chose to stay with you, didn't she?"

"But what if she loses?" Molly protested.

"You've worked hard and given her everything you could. Today most of it will be up to the Lady. Don't you think she deserves a chance to prove herself?"

"I just don't know," Molly said, stroking the filly absently. "I just want what's best for my Lady."

"You asked her."

Molly put her arms around the silky neck and hugged her horse. Lady rubbed her head on Molly's back. "She's happy here right now," Molly said, "but what about the noise and the crowds? She might not be so happy then."

"She'll be afraid — so are you. But you

can overcome it. That'll be the test, for Lady and you. That's what you have to face."

Molly and Dan stood looking at each other for a few minutes. For the first time Molly felt shut away from Dan's understanding. Up in her room, when she'd thought about setting Lady free, she'd expected Dan to know how she felt and to agree with her; now she felt betrayed. Then, because she was no longer sure what she should do, she buckled the halter on Lady, led her back into the stall, and finished her morning chores.

When she got back to the house for breakfast, there was a big box sitting on her plate. "What's this?" she asked, feeling embarrassed by her parents' wide smiles.

"Open it and see," her mother said.

Molly lifted the lid cautiously and was surprised to see a new pair of forest-green saddle pants and a coral and green plaid shirt. "But . . . I mean . . . Gee, they're beautiful! but . . ." she sputtered.

"They're for you to wear today, dear. A surprise from us." Her mother lifted the shirt out so she could see the stitching that marked the yoke and edged the cuffs.

"Oh, thank you. Thank you so much."

Molly felt tears stinging her eyes again. "They're beautiful."

"Eat your breakfast, then you can put them on," her father said. "We'll have to get an early start if we want to get Lady out to the fairgrounds before we go to town to see the parade."

"Yes, Daddy." Molly ate quickly, but without really tasting the food. She kept trying to believe that it would work out, that Lady was going to be all right. Hope and worry fought inside her, and she was both glad and sorry that Lady had refused to accept her gift of freedom. It proved her love and trust, but it also could cost Lady her life.

The clothes fit perfectly. When she paused in front of the mirror to look at herself, she felt almost equal to meeting the other contestants and competing in front of the crowd. Her father called to her from the yard, and Molly saw that he had already backed the double horse trailer up to the barn door. She hurried out to get the filly loaded.

As soon as Lady reached the barn door and saw the big yellow horse trailer, she balked. Molly stopped and let her look it over for a few minutes, then tried to lead her forward. One step and Lady halted again. This time Molly turned her around in a circle, trying to divert her attention, but as soon as Lady saw the trailer ahead of her, she refused to move.

"Want me to help?" her father asked.

Molly shook her head, knowing that her father would only force and frighten Lady, making her fight even harder. "Maybe it would be better if you moved the trailer away from the door, Daddy," she suggested. "Then she can get outside and see it better."

He groaned, but went out, and in a moment she heard the car start and the trailer disappeared from view. As soon as the motor stopped, she led Lady to the door. The filly followed easily now that the door wasn't blocked, but as soon as she saw the trailer again she shied.

The battle raged for almost twenty minutes. Molly made absolutely no progress. Lady simply refused to be coaxed close enough to the trailer even to see that it wouldn't hurt her. Finally Molly gave up and leaned against the barn. "I guess we should have tried loading her before," she said sadly. "But I didn't even think of it."

"Well, we've got to do something before very long. It's getting late." Her father's impatience was growing with every unsuccessful try.

"How about a blindfold?" Molly suggested. "Maybe if she couldn't see it — "

"Let's try." Her father got a clean cloth from the feed room and Molly knotted it over the bewildered filly's eyes.

Lady walked cautiously now, relying entirely on Molly, jumping at every sound.

As soon as her front hoof touched the slanted ramp of the trailer she tried to pull away. Molly held her, trying to drag her forward. Baron barked his encouragement from the back porch. Lady turned her blindfolded head his way and Molly had another inspiration.

"Daddy," she said, "maybe if Baron got in the trailer first, she wouldn't be so scared."

"It's worth a try, I guess," he said. In answer to his whistle Baron came loping up to Molly and Lady.

The two animals touched noses and Baron whined softly as though to comfort the frightened horse. "In the trailer, Baron," Molly ordered.

Baron bounded up the ramp and into one of the two stalls. Molly pulled on Lady's halter and very slowly the filly moved onto the ramp. Every step required more coaxing and Baron's encouraging whines, but at last Lady was in the other stall.

"Shall we leave Baron with her?" Molly asked. "Maybe he can calm her down."

"I suppose so. We can leave him in the car out there. You'd better tie her down and then take the blindfold off. I'll go get your mother and Dan."

"Sure, Daddy." Molly hurried, glad that Lady was finally ready to go. The filly shuddered when she saw where she was, but the rope on her halter kept her from trying to back out, or rear, and after a few minutes she settled down.

Her immediate problems solved, Molly began to think about the contest. In her mind she ran over the rules again and again. She didn't want to make some foolish mistake that would ruin the filly's chances forever. All the way to town she tried to concentrate, but her fears were in the front of her mind, crowding out everything else.

When they reached the fairgrounds, it was obvious that they would have no privacy in which to calm the filly. Though it was still three hours till the first event was scheduled, the entire area was swarming with life. Cars and horse trailers were scattered over the parking area behind the grandstand, and dozens of riders were racing around on the track and raising clouds of dust as they practiced in the arena.

Half a dozen small booths, selling food and souvenirs, had been set up behind the grandstand. Dogs and children raced around the booths, barking and screaming. Flags waved and snapped from the top of the grandstand and at various other points around the arena. There were so many people, so much noise and confusion, that Molly felt swallowed up by it. "Oh, Dan," she choked. He patted her hand gently as if he were soothing a nervous horse.

Her father drove halfway through the parking lot before he stopped the car. "We'll leave the trailer here, then go downtown for the parade," he said.

"You go ahead, Daddy," Molly said. "I think I'll stay here with Lady. She'll be so scared with all the noise and everything."

"Don't be silly. She has to get used to it," her father said.

"I know, but I'd rather stay here with her, please." Molly climbed up on the side of the trailer, high enough to see the filly's wildly rolling eyes.

"I'll stay too," Dan said. "I've seen enough parades."

"Well, if I'd known nobody wanted to see the parade, we could have waited till later to come." Her father slammed the car door and stood glaring around.

"Did I say I didn't want to see it?" her mother said, winking at Molly. "Get this car unhitched and we'll go."

It worked like magic. Her father whistled as he unhooked the trailer and even offered to stop by the announcer's booth to pick up Molly's number so she wouldn't have to go after it. Molly gave her mother a grateful hug before her parents drove away.

"Well," Molly said, turning back to Dan, "what'll we do now? Shall I take her out, or is she better off in the trailer for a while?"

"There's no telling how she feels about the trailer after riding in it, but I think the sooner she sees everything, the better. It won't be easy no matter how long we wait."

Molly nodded. Fear and nervousness were knotting her insides and she knew the filly would sense it. The training she'd given Lady in the peaceful pasture seemed far away and completely inadequate for the test that lay ahead. If Lady panicked at the sight of the horse trailer, what chance had she here? Molly helped Dan drop the tail-gate ramp. She ordered Baron out of the trailer, then climbed in to talk to Lady.

The filly was trembling. Her ears were back and her eyes rolled wild and white-rimmed. Except for the halter, she looked like a mustang fresh from the range. Molly took her time, petting and talking to Lady until some of the tension eased out of the slender body. Then she untied the rope and slowly backed the filly down the ramp.

As soon as her feet hit solid ground, Lady tried to break away. Dan came to Molly's aid, adding his weight to hers, and pulled the straining filly to a stop. They quickly tied her to the trailer and stood looking at each other.

"I've never seen her this way," Molly said. "She's half crazy."

"The ride didn't help. If we could have brought her in yesterday and given her a chance to get used to everything . . ." Dan's voice trailed off.

"Do you think she will get used to it?" Molly asked.

"She'll have to. Sit down now, you and the dog. Let her see you're not afraid. That might help."

Molly sat, but she knew the filly wouldn't be fooled. Molly was afraid and Lady could sense it. Only Baron seemed unimpressed by the crowds around them. He stretched out in the shadow of the trailer and went to sleep.

Dan brought a pail of water up from one of the booths and then got a small box of oats out of the trailer storage area. The filly sniffed them, but was too nervous to eat or drink. She shifted from side to side, dancing and pulling at her tie rope. In a few moments, her sides were wet with sweat.

"Do you think she'd be better off if I rode her?" Molly asked after a fretful half hour had passed.

Dan sighed. "It's worth a try, but be careful. She's getting worse instead of better."

His words didn't help. Molly had been hoping that her suspicions about Lady's nerves were wrong. She got the bridle and saddle from the trailer, and with Dan's help got them on the fidgeting horse. For the first time she hesitated to mount. She had never been afraid of Lady before, only of what might scare her. But now, here, she was frightened of her.

"Don't try to ride her anywhere in particular at first," Dan cautioned. "Just do your best to keep her under control. Let her go where she wants to as long as she'll go slow and easy. I'll hold her while you mount."

Molly nodded and tried to speak around the knot of fear in her throat, but no words came. Finally, she took a deep breath, gathered her reins tight, and swung up. With Dan holding her head, Lady could do little more than bounce, but Molly felt stiff and strange in the saddle and Lady's slightest movement jarred her. "I'm set, Dan," she choked, and he stepped away from the filly's head.

As expected Lady tried to run, but Molly's tight hold on the reins stopped her. Then she reared, fighting for her head. Molly leaned forward, standing in the stirrups to keep Lady from throwing herself over backward; she loosened the reins a little. Lady came down and tried again to run. The battle raged for what seemed hours. Molly's arms ached from the strain of holding the horse, and the filly's neck was white with foam, where the reins rubbed on her sweat-soaked hide.

Then just when Molly had reached the point of giving up, Lady stopped. She stood about three yards from the trailer, trembling so hard that it made Molly's teeth chatter. That broke the spell, and with it the tension that had made Molly feel like a stranger to her own horse. Sobbing with pity, she dropped the reins that she'd been fighting so long to hold, and leaned forward to hug Lady and let her know that the terrible fight was over for her too.

"I'm sorry, Lady," she sobbed. "I never should have made you come here. I should have known better. I love you, Lady, I never wanted to hurt you this way."

The filly looked around, and Molly cried even harder when she saw the flecks of blood on the corners of the filly's mouth. She slid off the horse and led her over to the pail of water so she could sponge out her sore mouth. Then she stood, just talking and stroking Lady until the filly's coat dried and her trembling stopped.

"I think the worst is over," Dan said, snapping Molly back to reality.

"Oh, Dan, how could I have done that to her? Why didn't you stop me?" Molly demanded.

"You did it to yourselves. Look at your hands, Molly."

Molly looked down and was surprised to find welts on her palms and fingers. She didn't remember hurting herself while she fought to control the filly.

"You were fighting each other and your own fears at the same time," Dan said. "You won together. Now go get yourself cleaned up — there'll be a place under the grandstand — and I'll sponge some of the sweat stains off the filly. Your folks will be back before long and it would be better if they saw you riding around quietly."

"Do you really think she'll be okay now?" Molly asked, remembering that the greatest test was still ahead; the battle they'd just waged was only the beginning.

"The worst is over, I'm sure of that. We can hope and you can do your best — that's all. Now go."

As Molly walked down the slope toward the grandstand, she realized how much the crowd had increased. A long line of cars waited to enter the gate of the fairgrounds, which were used each year for the gymkhana. The parade must be over, she decided, and that meant it wouldn't be long before the first event was announced.

When Molly looked into the mirror, she understood why Dan had insisted she wash before her parents saw her. She had bitten her lip sometime during her battle with Lady and the blood was caked around her mouth. Her clothes were spotted with foam from the horse and, of course, her hands looked bad.

Molly took her time washing up. She tried to keep calm and remain sure of Lady as she thought of the soon-to-begin gymkhana. She almost hated to go back to the trailer. It would be easier just to load Lady and go home — but her father had said that Lady couldn't go back without a ribbon. Molly knew he would never understand that Lady had already met a big test — she hadn't run away even though Molly had dropped the reins to hug her.

Molly was halfway up the hill when a familiar voice called to her.

She turned and saw a tall, quiet pinto, then she recognized Ginger, smiling down at her from his back. "Hi," she said, smiling back. "That's a pretty horse."

"Thanks. Did you bring your filly in?"

Molly nodded, feeling shy even though she liked Ginger. "She's up at the trailer," she explained.

"Want a lift up there?" Ginger asked. "Old Duke carries double."

"Thanks a lot." Molly climbed up behind Ginger.

"Did you enter anything?" Ginger asked.

"Three events, but I'm worried about Lady. She's so scared of everything."

"That's right — you did say you were just breaking her, didn't you."

"She's fine at the ranch, but crowds scare her." Molly didn't add that they scared her too. She was sure Ginger wouldn't understand. "That's Lady over there," she said.

"She sure is small, almost pony size," Ginger said, sliding to the ground. "She's built like a thoroughbred though. What is she, anyway?" Ginger approached the filly quietly but without hesitation, and Molly was pleased to see that Lady wasn't afraid of her.

"She was with a wild herd, so I don't know anything about her parents. But she's as fast as a racehorse."

"Gee." Ginger's glance was admiring. "How did you catch her?"

"I . . . a . . ." Just then they were interrupted by the raucous squealing of the public-address system and a blaring announcement.

"Oh, they're calling the drill team," Ginger said. "That means me too. I'll talk to you down at the arena, okay? Good luck with your filly."

"Good luck to you too," Molly called as Ginger rode away. She felt a little better as she checked the cinch of her saddle, then examined Lady's mouth to make sure the bit wasn't touching any of the sore spots.

Dan came around the trailer. "Ready to take her down to look around?" he asked.

Molly nodded, untying the filly and turning her toward the arena. "I hope she's okay now. I mean, when the folks get back, I want her to look calm."

"Just keep calm yourself and you'll make it." Dan stood at Lady's head while Molly mounted, but he didn't try to hold her this time.

Lady started off quickly, trying to move away from the hubbub, but she didn't fight when Molly reined her around and headed her back past the trailer. She was still afraid, Molly could feel it in the way she moved, but her blind panic was gone. Slowly, she angled Lady down the hill toward the arena.

The crowd seemed to thicken the nearer they came to the grandstand, and the more people there were around them, the more slowly Lady moved. Molly didn't hurry her, and she felt her hopes growing with every step the filly took. If Lady didn't panic, Molly felt they had a chance.

They rode all the way around the arena, behind the chutes, and across the racetrack, which was blocked off now by the side-arena fences. Molly stopped to inspect the two gates that were being used as arena entrances.

Twice, strange noises frightened Lady and she tried to bolt, but each time, after a few frantic bounds, Molly was able to control her and turn her back. It was a long ride, and Molly was glad when they reached the other side of the grandstand and she could turn Lady away from the thickest part of the crowd and lope up the hill to the trailer, where her parents were waiting.

"Well," her father said, "I see you've got everything under control here. You should have come with us after all — it was a good parade."

"I'll bet," Molly agreed, grateful that her parents hadn't witnessed her earlier ride.

"We've been busy here, though."

"Want a hot dog before the gymkhana starts?" her mother asked.

"I don't think so," Molly said, dismounting. "I'm too excited to be hungry. Did you get my number?"

"Right here. Your lucky number — twenty-seven." Her mother took the safety pins out of the oilcloth and started pinning it to the back of Molly's shirt.

"I hope it is lucky," Molly said, her eyes meeting Dan's.

The loudspeaker began crackling again. "Put Baron in the car and let's go find some seats," her father said. "And you'd better get down there too. The barrel-and-stake race is the first event — right after the drill-team grand entry."

"Good luck!" they all three called as Molly mounted Lady again. She tried to wave, but her hands were shaking so, she almost dropped the reins. Music blared from the loudspeaker as she rode down the hill. Molly saw Paul on his black quarter horse entering the arena with the drill team. The gymkhana had begun!

Chapter 16

Molly reined in a little way back from the east gate and settled down to watch the drill team. Ginger waved to her as she and Duke swung by, and Molly saw a very superior looking Robin, in the pivot position, carrying a flag and riding a gorgeous palomino.

The drill was fast and complicated, but everyone seemed to know exactly what to do. Molly felt a pang of envy as she watched, for the riders were all relaxed and seemed to be having a lot of fun. Until Lady had entered her life, Molly hadn't thought of riding as being fun, but now she realized that she had been missing a lot.

For the drill finale, Robin and Paul "rode the colors" at a full gallop around the other members of the team, who sat quietly, hats off, while the National Anthem was played.

As soon as the drill team rode out of the arena through the west gate, six sets of barrels were set up for the first event. The under-twelve section was called first, and Molly watched closely as five young riders competed wildly. The lanes were close together, and several of the riders spent most of their time fighting their horses. Only three of the five riders managed to carry all six stakes from one barrel to the other.

The juniors were next, and Molly listened for her number. It was announced third, which put her right in the middle, a position she hadn't wanted. She turned Lady into line behind a stocky bay, and the filly began to dance, pulling at the reins and fighting to turn away from the arena.

"Where'd you find that peanut?" a taunting voice asked.

Molly turned and saw Robin right behind her on the fancy palomino.

"Hi," Molly said coolly.

"Is it a pony?" Robin asked nastily.

"*She's* a mustang," Molly said, concentrating on getting Lady lined up beside the empty barrel and facing the barrel with the stakes that waited across the arena.

Robin, who had been given the position on Molly's left, made another nasty comment that Molly couldn't quite hear. She tried to keep calm and concentrate on what she and Lady must do. But her heart was pounding so hard she barely heard the gun until Lady leaped forward.

In a few seconds they were streaking by the second barrel. Molly fought Lady around, pulled her to a stop beside the barrel, and picked up her first stake. They were behind the other contestants because of Lady's near runaway, but as soon as Molly had the stake in her hand, Lady seemed to settle down.

She raced back to the starting barrel and cut so close around it that Molly had no trouble dropping the stake in. Lady headed back for the second stake, her speed quickly bringing her even with the other contestants. By the third stake they were clearly ahead of all the other riders except Robin and her well-trained palomino. Lady was faster than Robin's horse, but she still shied or ran wide when anything startled her, and they lost precious time as Molly fought to bring her back into line.

The girl on Molly's right was having trouble with her horse too. As Molly and Lady headed back with their fourth stake, the heavy bay came crashing toward them, the rider swinging her stake wildly. Lady spun away, cutting close to the palomino and bringing a shout of fury from Robin.

Molly tried to hold Lady and ease her back, but it was hopeless as long as she could use only one hand. Regretfully, she dropped her stake and used both hands to pull the frightened filly into a tight circle until she was under control again. By that time the other contestants had completed the event. Molly rode out sadly, knowing that she had only two chances left.

"Just watch out, peanut," a nasty voice said. "Next time you get in my way, I'll ride right over you."

"You couldn't get close unless I waited for you," Molly shouted back, her will to win returning. The first loss wasn't Lady's fault; she'd done her best. It was bad luck, but they'd do better, Molly was sure of that.

She stopped Lady near the fence, forcing

her to stand and watch the activity in the arena. At first Lady danced and tried to pull away, but after a while she accepted it and left Molly free to watch the other contestants in their events.

Everyone seemed to be having fun. Even the adults were shouting and laughing and acting silly. Robin had won a blue ribbon for the barrel-and-stake race and she earned red and white ones later, which she fastened on the palomino's bridle.

Molly looked around for Ginger and Paul as Lady settled down and gave her time to think. She felt like a lonely outsider; everyone was laughing and talking and seemed to know everyone else.

Molly was standing in her stirrups scanning the grandstand, trying to spot her parents, when the loudspeaker called her number. A quick glance at the arena told her why — the men were readying the arena for the pole-bending contest. She headed for the gate as quickly as she could, but she was still the last rider into the arena.

Since there were more riders than there were lines of poles, the entrants were divided into two groups of six riders each. Molly rode off to one side with the second group, pleased to see that Ginger was in her section. Robin was in the first group.

"Hi," Ginger said. "How're you doing?"

"Okay, I guess," Molly said. "How about you?"

"Nothing to brag about. I picked up a yellow in the potato race and a red in rescue with Dave, but I can't seem to get old Duke in gear today."

"It sure looks like everyone is having fun."

"That's what this is for," Ginger said. "You're supposed to be having fun. Is this your first time at a gymkhana?"

Molly nodded, her eyes on the riders now lining up for the race. The starting line was back a little from the first pole and she could see the timekeepers across from the starting line. Molly was trying to puzzle out why they weren't at the starting line, when the gun sounded.

Robin's palomino broke first and started through the poles a little ahead of the other horses. Molly leaned forward, watching as the golden horse snaked through the poles, spun around the end one, and headed back through the poles again. Another quick turn and he was well ahead on his third run-through. Robin galloped across the finish line an easy winner of the first section.

"Wow," Molly said, hating herself for the awe in her voice.

"I hate her for that," Ginger said calmly. "She just doesn't deserve a horse like Delight."

"He is a beauty," Molly agreed. "Did she train him herself?"

"Are you kidding? Her father hired a man to train the horse. It took him longer to teach her to ride Delight than it did to train the horse. She couldn't teach a mouse to eat cheese."

Molly laughed but had no time to comment before their group was called to line up. This time she felt more confident. Lady was less afraid now, and she had been very good at pole bending on the practice course at home. They lined up next to Ginger.

At the crack of the gun, Lady leaped forward and headed around the first pole. As Molly had expected, Lady's small size was an asset, for the poles were spaced to accommodate big horses. Molly had scarcely caught her breath before Lady was spinning around the end pole and heading back. It wasn't till they weaved their way around the starting pole again that Molly realized her mistake.

She tried to slow Lady a little so she could turn her to go through the poles for a third time, but the filly remembered her training and raced for the starting line, as they had always done at the ranch. By the time Molly got Lady turned back for a third run through the poles, even her speed couldn't bring her across the finish line better than third. Molly knew third was not good enough to qualify for a ribbon since the winners would be taken from both sections according to their times.

"What happened?" Ginger asked as they rode back.

"I didn't know the race was three times through the poles. We practiced just twice, and Lady didn't understand." Molly could hardly choke back the tears.

"They changed the rules. You didn't know? They thought it would be more difficult if the horses had to make two of those full turns. That's really tough luck. You had it won easily."

"I'm glad you won our section," Molly said, trying not to think about Lady's one remaining hope. Only the barrel race was left — the event they'd practiced the least. It seemed hopeless.

"When they announce the times, I'll know

where I finished in the whole race," Ginger said. "Duke's usually better on the barrels than he is on the poles, so I'll be satisfied with second. At least, I'm pretty sure Robin had better time than I did."

The winning numbers were announced and Molly watched while Ginger collected a red, and Robin took the blue. If only she'd had more time, Molly thought, even a few more weeks might have made all the difference. Or if she'd known about the rule change so she could have worked with Lady. It wasn't fair to put Lady against these experienced, well-trained horses. But if she didn't get a ribbon, Lady would not be going back to the ranch with them — fair or not.

"Congratulations, Ginger," Molly said as they rode out of the arena together.

"Thanks, but I wish it had been you and me picking up the ribbons. Robin is getting so stuck-up nobody can talk to her. She already told me I could forget the blue in barrel racing. Seems Delight is tops at that as well as everything else."

"I'd be happy with any ribbon, believe me," Molly said. "When is the barrel racing?" she asked.

"There are so many contestants, it'll be

the last event. Are you in that too?"

Molly nodded, wishing now that she'd chosen a different contest, something less popular. Out at the ranch the boot race, potato race, and egg race had sounded pretty silly, but now she wished she'd entered; three chances were not enough, not when Lady's very life depended on winning a ribbon.

"Don't look so scared, there's always next year. That little filly of yours is the fastest thing I've ever seen," Ginger said.

"I hope she's fast enough. If she just doesn't get scared . . ." Molly let the sentence trail off.

"Why don't you ride last?" Ginger asked. "A lot of the contestants leave if they don't have qualifying times, so there won't be such a crowd at the gate."

"Do you think I could?" Molly asked. It would at least prolong the time before she and Lady had to meet this final test.

"I'll ask for you," Ginger said. "My uncle's the announcer's assistant, so he can just change your number to last. Be right back."

Molly tried to watch the activity in the arena, but fear crawled up and down her back and froze her stomach into an icy lump. She had little hope that they could sell the filly. Even though her speed was great, she was too small for most riders and her wildness was obvious. The cannery truck loomed up in Molly's mind. "Never, Lady," she whispered. "I'd run away and take you to the mountains so you'd be free. I won't let him sell you!" But she knew these were empty promises. Her father would fight any plan to save Lady.

She recognized Paul as he rode forward in the arena to receive a blue ribbon for the event that had just ended. Molly clapped for him, but her spirits didn't lift. She was tired, and she sensed that the many wild frights had taken their toll of Lady's energies too. Ginger came winding her way back through the crowd of riders, a wide smile on her face.

"You'll be last," she said.

"Thanks a lot." Molly forced a smile. "I really do appreciate it."

"Heck, I don't mind. I got my number changed. I'm just before you. I'd rather be toward the end. That way you know where you stand. If you don't make a good time, you know you're out."

They sat in comfortable silence, each busy with her own thoughts, but still not alone. Paul rode up beside Molly, a grin on his face and three blue ribbons fluttering on Pecos' bridle.

"Looks like you've had a good day," Molly said.

"Passable. You sure got some rough breaks, though. I watched you both times. You've done a good job on your Lady, but she still needs a lot of work if you want to make a gymkhana horse out of her."

"She's really a cow pony," Molly said, "and a good one too."

"You waiting for the barrel racing?" Paul asked.

"Are you in it?" Molly asked, hoping she wasn't going to have to compete against Pecos.

Paul shook his head. "Nope. I'm your cheering section for that event."

"We'll need it," Molly said, stroking Lady's neck with love and despair.

"You'll make it all right," Paul said, "Don't worry."

"I haven't done too well so far," Molly said.

"Then you're due for a win."

Chapter 17

As the arena was cleared after the next-to-last event, a few people left the grand-stand, and some of the contestants rode away. However, most remained, lining the fences to watch the barrel racing. The men in the arena put the barrels out in a tri-angular pattern and the west gate was closed. The east gate would serve as entry and exit for this event. Flags placed about ten feet inside the arena showed the timer's position and marked the start and finish of the cloverleaf barrel race.

Molly started to turn Lady away from the fence to go to the gate, but Ginger stopped her. "You might as well relax,

Molly, there are over twenty entries," she said. "Just sit tight and let Lady study the course."

Molly settled back, waiting for the first contestant to be called. It was good to be with company, almost friends, but they couldn't seem to lift the burden of her terror. She searched her mind for the words to tell them of her agreement with her father — of the only chance he'd given her to keep Lady, but shyness sealed her throat. They couldn't understand, she was sure. After a moment the loudspeaker blared and a girl on a tall black mare galloped between the flags and swirled around the first barrel. The last event had started.

At the second barrel the horse cut wide, losing ground, but the rider pulled her back and whipped her into the third barrel at top speed. She cut close on that one, then opened out to a full racing gallop toward the open gate. The timers checked watches and signaled the announcer. Her time was twenty seconds flat.

Molly let out the breath she'd been holding and looked over at Ginger. "Is that good?" she asked, wishing that she had some way of knowing how fast Lady had run on their practice field.

"About average for here. Last year's best time was seventeen point eight."

"Don't be so modest," Paul broke in. "Admit you set that record."

"Why tell anyone," Ginger said with a grin. "Then I just have to live up to it. Besides, I wouldn't be surprised if Robin's Delight cuts that down to seventeen flat. He's good, and he's fast."

"He's not that much faster than Duke," Paul argued.

Molly sat between them, not making any comment. As they talked, several more riders completed that cloverleaf pattern around the barrels. None of them bettered the twenty seconds, but all were quite close. All the riders lost time on the second barrel, which was a turn to the left, but made up most of their lost ground on the final dash to the gate. Molly noticed that the riders carried quirts and whipped every stride to the finish, much like racing jockeys.

The list of contestants continued to be called. One horse fell in the loose dirt behind the third barrel and the ambulance was summoned to pick up his motionless rider. The shrill siren as the ambulance spun out of the arena left a void of silence behind. For several minutes no contestant was called and the riders milled around.

Finally the race was resumed and a pretty blonde girl galloped into the ring aboard a small pinto. Molly could see the fear in the girl's face, and when her time was recorded, her nervousness showed. Her ride had taken almost twenty-four seconds. The next few rides were no better; then, as the memory of the fallen horse and rider faded, the pace quickened.

There were two nineteen-second rides and one nineteen point three, to eliminate all the earlier contestants. The crowd at the gate had thinned considerably, and there were more empty seats in the grandstand. Molly stared at the ripped-up brown earth where the horse had fallen. It hadn't been wearing shoes. Perhaps, she thought, a horse with shoes would be safer. Most of the horses here had been shod and Molly wished fervently that she had had Lady shod.

"We'd better get over there," Ginger said, breaking into Molly's worried thoughts. "There can't be more than a half dozen riders left to go."

"Okay," Molly said, her fingers stiff and cold on the reins.

As they rode away, Paul called, "Good luck, both of you. I'll be over to congratulate you."

At the gate there were only four riders waiting their turn. The next to the last one was Robin on the now ribbon-decked Delight. Ginger smiled and waved. Robin returned the smile with icy eyes. She looked so calm and sure, and Delight was well controlled but obviously eager for his try. Molly wished they didn't have to race him.

She held Lady well back from the other horses, letting Ginger ride Duke ahead of her. From where they sat, it was almost impossible to see the race, but the time of each rider was announced clearly, and as each girl rode forward, Molly came closer to that moment of decision.

The girl ahead of Robin was having trouble with her horse. When her turn came her horse bucked, then ran furiously out into the arena. Molly moved up to follow their progress, but several riders stood between her and the gate and she heard nothing but the roar of the crowd.

"That girl shouldn't be allowed to have a horse," Ginger said furiously. "That was last year's top barrel horse and look at him now."

"What happened?" Molly asked.

"She's been beating him around till he's half crazy. Look out!"

The warning came too late. Molly had turned at the violent clattering of hooves, but before she could get out of the way, the wild-eyed horse, coming out of the arena, crashed into Lady with the force of a runaway freight train. Molly felt an agonizing pain in her ankle, then she and the filly went rolling in the turf.

For a moment she lay still, letting the blackness clear from her eyes. Then worry about Lady made her drag herself painfully to her feet. The filly stood about a yard away, head up, eyes white-ringed by fear. Molly limped to her, caught the reins before she could bolt, and vaulted on, knowing that she couldn't hold the filly from the ground, not with a bad ankle.

"Are you all right?" Ginger asked, white-faced.

"I think so." Molly kept the reins tight as Lady crowhopped, and then tried to rear. Molly stayed on by gripping with her knees to hold her balance. After several jumps, Lady stopped and stood shivering. Molly stroked her shoulder gently, talking to her, trying to ease the knots of fear from her muscles.

"There goes Robin," Ginger said. Molly moved up to watch.

Robin leaned forward, her whip rising and falling across the golden haunches with every stride. Delight was beautiful to watch. He needed no guidance or urging as he spun around the barrels, losing little ground even on the difficult second barrel. Coming toward the finish, he put forth a tremendous burst of speed. Robin was smiling widely as she thundered through the open gate and yanked the big horse into a sliding stop.

All noise seemed to die when the loudspeaker crackled and the announcer's voice broke loudly around them. "Ladies and gentlemen," he said, "we have a new gymkhana record. Robin Taylor has run the barrels in sixteen point nine!"

There was a burst of applause from the grandstand, but it didn't drown out the sound of Robin's voice. "Well, Ginger," she said. "I guess that's a little too fast for your plug." She rode by Molly with only a pitying look.

Another contestant was called and made

an unimpressive ride. Then it was Ginger's turn. Molly rode closer to the gate to watch. The numbness of her fall was beginning to wear off, and behind it came a wake of pain. She slipped her feet into the stirrups, wincing. Her ankle was getting worse, it wouldn't even hold her weight when she tried to stand in the stirrups.

Ginger plunged out through the gate, hitting Duke only once to get him started, then leaning forward, half hidden by the pinto's flying mane. She hadn't exaggerated Duke's skill at barrel racing. He headed for the first barrel, cutting so close it rocked as he went by. The second was done almost as well, and he sped for the third in what Molly was sure must be record time.

Duke took the third tight turn with his usual ease, and added a surprising burst of speed as he headed for the gate. Molly's heart flared with pride in Ginger's performance even though she knew it cut farther into her chances of saving Lady from the terror of sale.

Ginger galloped by, eased Duke to a stop, then rode back to wait for the announcer to call her time. Molly's whole body felt cold and dead, except for her ankle which throbbed with every breath the filly took. She knew she couldn't make the ride with it that way. She unbuckled her belt and wrapped it around her leg, just above the ankle. Then she threaded it back through the stirrup leather before buckling it.

She pulled it tight, knowing she had to keep her foot in the stirrup on this ride, especially on the second turn, where her injured ankle would be on the inside. If her ankle was sprained, as she was sure it was, this was the only way to be sure she didn't lose the stirrup. If Lady fell, Molly would have no chance of rolling free. But she didn't care. Nothing was as important to her now as winning a ribbon, any ribbon, and keeping her horse.

"Well, we have another great time," the announcer boomed. "Ginger Kahn made the circuit in seventeen seconds flat."

Molly leaned down to check the belt around her leg and then saw it. Just above Lady's hock a wide red gash shone wet against the dark hide. Blood was running slowly down the filly's leg and the ground around her hoof was wet with it.

"Our last contestant today will be Molly

Rogers riding Prairie Lady." The announcer's voice boomed and the way to the gate was cleared for her.

Molly straightened up, afraid and sick with indecision.

The cut was an ugly one and in a bad spot. Should she pull out and try to explain to her father? Or would he just remember the other mistakes Lady had made and get rid of her anyway? And if she did enter the arena, what would the strain of the barrel race do to Lady's leg? The picture of Lady, crippled, rose in her mind and Molly lifted her reins, ready to turn away.

"What's the matter?" a nasty voice asked. "Lose your peanut starter? Let me help you." Robin brought her quirt down cruelly on the unsuspecting Lady's haunches.

Molly and Lady leaped into the arena in a violent burst of speed. Leaning forward, Molly made no attempt to guide Lady. It took all her strength just to stay in the saddle. Every stride jarred her ankle and threatened to tear her leg loose from the belt.

Lady's stride was a little rough as she turned into the first barrel, but she seemed to have forgotten the pain and fright of the blow and was settling down to the race like a veteran. She came so close that Molly's knee brushed the first barrel, rocking it a little. Her stride became more uneven as she headed for the second barrel, but Molly had no chance to rein in and stop the torture.

Lady spun around the second barrel. Molly's full weight pressed on her injured ankle. She nearly screamed with pain. Her leg flopped away from the filly's side, knocking against the barrel and leaving it rocking.

Grimly, Molly set her teeth in her lower lip, biting hard to keep the pain in her ankle from driving her into unconsciousness. She tasted blood as Lady skidded around the third barrel, and she felt the filly shudder as she strained her injured leg. Molly forced herself forward, riding as high on Lady's withers as she could to keep her weight off the horse's injured leg. Lady galloped a little awkwardly, but gave a gallant final burst of speed as she headed for the gate.

As they passed through the opening, Molly's swollen ankle flopped loose and hit the gatepost a glancing blow. A fresh wave of pain ripped up from her leg and blackness followed it. Molly didn't even have time to pull Lady to a halt before her face hit the filly's mane and the world faded.

Molly felt the hard ground and tried to open her eyes. Memory flooded in and she struggled to sit up. "Lady?" she gasped. "Is Lady all right?"

"Take it easy," a familiar voice said, and Molly turned to see Dan kneeling beside her. "Your Lady's okay." He pointed and Molly saw that Paul was examining Lady's hind leg while Ginger held the trembling filly's head.

"I've got to help . . ." Molly tried to get up, but a stab of pain from her ankle made her flop back against Dan.

"She's okay," he said again. "Just lie still."

"What happened?" Molly asked. "Did I lose?"

"Lose?" Ginger's bright voice came from the filly's side. "You just beat me out of second place. On four good legs this filly would have whipped Delight too. She was great and so were you, and I for one am reporting Robin to the judges for what she did."

Molly scarcely heard the last words. "I'll get a ribbon?" she asked, relief and pain filling her eyes with tears.

"A bright-red one," Paul said. "Now for Heaven's sake relax. The cut's not too bad, but you'll both be limping around for a while."

Molly stopped struggling as she remembered her exit from the arena. "How'd you get here so fast, Dan?" she asked.

"I was wondering why your number was changed. I just came to see what was up. Then, when I came up to the gates, I saw Lady tearing out of the arena and you flopping down on her neck like a sack of grain."

Molly took a deep breath. "I guess I must have blacked out," she said, weakly.

"You're one lucky girl! You slid clear off Lady and were hanging under her belly by the time I got to you. She just stood still so she wouldn't step on you. I've never seen anything like it."

Molly heard her parents' voices and struggled to sit up. They were running and she saw plainly the worry and fear written on their faces. Fresh tears rolled down her cheeks as she thought of Lady — fighting her fear to stand and protect her.

"What happened?" her father asked.

"We won a ribbon," Molly said, her heart too full of love and pride to tell him the rest right then.

"Oh, baby, why did you do it? What happened to you?" her mother asked. "We could tell something was wrong the moment you rode into the arena."

Slowly, with help from Ginger and Paul, Molly explained about the runaway and Lady's fall, her ankle and the filly's cut leg, and Robin's final act of cruelty. Then Molly listened, feeling proud and humble, as Dan told her parents what happened after she blacked out.

"Any other horse would have panicked and killed her," he said. "Lady's love for Molly made her stand still, though I'd guess she was more frightened than she'd ever been in her life."

Molly's parents were furious when they learned she had tied her foot in the stirrup, but Molly scarcely heard them. Ginger had gone out to the arena to receive her yellow ribbon and came back with the red ribbon too. She handed it to Molly with a smile.

"Next year it'll be a blue for sure," she said.

"Next year," Molly agreed, feeling the warmth of friendship as she looked up at Ginger.

The crowd cleared away while the doctor checked her ankle, but both Ginger and Paul waited until he pronounced it a bad sprain, but not broken. Then Ginger said, "I know you'll have to stay in bed for a couple of days, but as soon as you can hobble, come to town and see me."

"Maybe you could come out," Molly said. "I'd love to show you the ranch. I mean, if you'd like to see it."

"I'd love to," Ginger said. "Maybe I can talk Mom into bringing me."

"If you wouldn't mind showing the place to two guests, my brother works a couple of miles east of your ranch," Paul said, looking a little shy. "He could bring us out."

"I'd like both of you to come," Molly said, wincing as the doctor began wrapping her ankle.

"How about Wednesday?" Molly's mother broke in. "I'll give you our phone number and you can call and let us know if you can come."

Molly smiled at her mother, then turned

her eyes on Dan, who was unsaddling Lady. "Is she really all right, Dan?" she asked.

He turned and nodded, a tiny smile of pride touched his face and lit up his eyes. Molly closed her eyes for a moment, thinking of the future — rides with Ginger and Paul, other gymkhanas, even high school — it seemed less frightening now.

"Paul," she said, holding out the ribbon, "would you put it on Lady's bridle for me, please."

"Sure," he said. "She's earned it."

Lady lifted her head and the red ribbon fluttered in the prairie wind. The white was gone from her eyes. She limped over to Molly and lowered her delicate head to whicker softly and nuzzle Molly's cheek. "It's all right, girl," Molly said. "You're mine now — forever."